I0778388

JACQUI BLEU, BOUNTY HUNTER

ELIZABETH ANNE GREY

This book is a work of fiction. All names, places, characters, and events are products of the author's imagination and are fictitious. Any similarities to actual events, places, people, living or dead, is coincidental.

Copyright 2024 by Elizabeth Anne Grey

Cover Design | Editing | Book Design & Typesetting
Enchanted Ink Publishing

Dark Citrine LLC

First Edition:

ISBN: 978-1-7378365-9-9 (Hardcover)
ISBN: 979-8-9910336-0-2 (E-Book)

Dark Citrine LLC
PO Box 3563
Arlington, WA 98223

www.darkcitrine.net

For information about upcoming books written by Elizabeth Anne Grey, you can follow Elizabeth Anne Grey on Facebook, @darkcitrinewriter on TikTok, and @darkcitrinellc on Instagram.

Printed in the United States of America

Earl Edward Grey, I miss you every day.

ELIZABETH ANNE GREY

JACQUI BLEU, BOUNTY HUNTER

Who's a girl gotta kill
to make a buck?

PROLOGUE

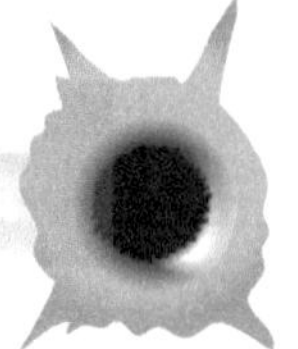

SHOTS WERE FIRED, AND SCREAMS WERE HEARD COMING from downstairs. Whoever they were, they were making their way through the house and they were being thorough. A young mother held her child against her chest as she moved quickly upstairs through the master bedroom and into her private bath. Her silky rose-colored robe flowed behind her as her upswept red locks cascaded loosely around her panicked face.

"We *must* hurry!"

A scared nanny raced to keep up, following her into the bathroom.

"Please, you *must* take her," the mother pleaded. "You must save my daughter!"

"But I have no money and *I'm* not . . ." She paused, staring at the woman. "She needs *you*."

"If she stays, they will kill her." The mother pressed the bundled infant into the nanny's arms. "Emma, *please*."

The young woman took the child, glancing around the beautiful bathroom decorated with beige marble flooring and soft neutral tones. It was elegant like the rest of the house, which was a perfect reflection of the DeMotts. She looked back at Mrs. DeMott, the woman who'd employed her for the past year, who'd always been kind and generous. In that moment, scared or not, Emma knew what she had to do.

"Okay." She exhaled. "I will save your daughter." Her brown eyes were on the verge of spilling tears.

"Thank you." Mrs. DeMott reached out and caressed the girl's face, her own unshed tears glistening in her light-blue eyes.

Mrs. DeMott turned, her bare feet making soft slapping noises with every step as she hurried across the cold floor. Emma followed her with the sleeping baby in her arms but jumped, glancing back at the doorway when she heard another gunshot. She shuffled forward, still looking behind her, and when she turned, she saw Mrs. DeMott was now on the other side of the room. Emma wondered for a moment what she was doing, and then she saw Mrs. DeMott reach inside and up on the front wall of the niche, her arm moving downward as if pulling something. A moment later, a motorized mechanism could be heard behind the wall, and Emma stepped back when a panel slid up, revealing what looked to be an old dumbwaiter.

She took a step forward, cradling the baby, and looked past Mrs. DeMott into the shadows of the small car, where she saw a medium-size bag pushed to the rear wall on the right.

"Emma, listen to me. We haven't much time. Ride the car all the way down to the ground floor and then wait until you hear nothing but silence." She pointed just inside the opening of the car. "There is a lever on the front wall on the right here that will open the door when you're ready. The cover of night should help conceal you when you leave. That bag in the corner contains keys to a car parked in the back shed and plenty of money to take care of my baby girl and yourself."

Mrs. DeMott took the baby back into her arms for a moment, holding the sleeping child while Emma climbed inside the small space and glanced around, detecting the faint odor of degreaser.

"Goodbye, my beautiful girl, my Jacqueline Indigo." Mrs. DeMott leaned down and kissed her three-day-old daughter on the forehead as new tears fell down her flushed cheeks. Reluctantly, she handed the baby back to Emma, caressing the young woman's face. "Please take care of her as if she were your own," she whispered. "Now, *go.*"

Emma nodded, holding the baby against her chest as the front wall slid down and she was engulfed in darkness. She felt a shift in the car after hearing a motor in the wall come to life, and she focused on staying calm, hoping the child would remain asleep. The car slowly moved downward, and she jumped when she heard angry voices in the bathroom above her.

"Where is the child?" a gruff man's voice demanded.

"She is dead. Died just after she was born." Mrs. DeMott stood proudly in front of the angry intruder. "Where's my husband?"

"Don't worry, honey. You're about to join him."

Mrs. DeMott's screams echoed against the marble, causing tears to spring to Emma's eyes. She closed them tightly as the sounds of gunshots made her instinctively hold the baby tighter to her chest, rocking to soothe herself and the sleeping child.

The car slowed and finally stopped when it reached the bottom. Emma exhaled, listening for any sounds that would tell her where the bad men were, but she couldn't hear anything. She gingerly slid back into the car until she could comfortably lean against the rear wall. She gently rocked the baby in her arms when the child stirred a bit, then settled back down. Emma closed her own eyes, taking deep breaths as more tears rolled down her cheeks. She prayed whoever was still in the house would leave soon so she and the baby could escape. She exhaled loudly as exhaustion overtook her.

Emma jumped suddenly when she heard the sound of multiple car doors slamming shut, finding solace when the roar of the engines faded into the night.

The baby awoke, acting fussy.

"I know, little one," she whispered, gently rocking her again. "We'll go soon, and then I can get you something to eat."

Emma waited a little longer, listening and staring into the darkness all around her. She sighed and reached out to locate the lever on the wall. When she found it, she stopped and listened one last time. Silence.

She flipped the lever, and the front wall slid up to reveal a narrow, dimly lit space. She set the baby down to her left inside the compartment and moved forward, dropping her legs over the edge. She leaned forward, pleased to discover she was in a small closet downstairs in the basement where some of the Christmas decorations were stored. She sighed, thinking about how different the holidays would be this year. She slid towards the opening and reached behind her, pulling the bag toward the front, thankful the weight of it wasn't too heavy. She located car keys and a small flashlight in a side pocket. She unzipped the bag and was happy to discover a full bottle and an ice pack to keep the milk inside fresh. She zipped up the bag and stood, turning and placing her right knee just inside the car to pick the baby up. Jacqueline's little eyes opened, and their indigo color took Emma's breath away. New tears fell at the thought of this child never knowing her parents and what they sacrificed to keep her alive.

Emma composed herself and pulled the bag out, hoisting the strap up over her shoulder. She turned and walked toward the front of the small nook, pausing another moment before stepping out of the closet. She walked to the outside door and noticed the sun had long gone down, and she was grateful for the flashlight. She hit the button on the end to light her way, moving quickly up the small inclined path away from the house and toward the shed. She hesitated a moment when the rustle of the trees filled the night air, causing her heart to pound even harder than it already was.

She opened the doors to the shed, shining the flashlight around the space to make sure her path was clear. The back wall was decorated with different gardening tools, while the smell of potting soil and dirt overwhelmed her senses, stirring memories of her own childhood. She hit the button a couple of times on the key fob and moved to the passenger side of the vehicle, opening the door. She set the bag on the floor and wondered for a moment how she was going to secure the child. She looked back at the rear wall of the shed and noticed a large box and a blanket on the counter. She carefully laid the baby on the seat, positioning the bag next to the child to secure her in place for a moment. Emma moved to the back of the shed and grabbed the box and blanket. She shook the blanket out, then rolled it lengthwise, lining the inside of the box. She froze when she heard the trees rustle loudly outside, realizing she needed to hurry. She walked back to the open passenger door of the car and moved the bag back down to the floor. She set the box on the seat, carefully laying the baby inside and pushing the box against the back of the seat. She closed the passenger door and moved around to the driver's side, climbed in, and turned the engine over. She reached down and removed the full bottle of milk from inside the bag, propping it up with the end of the blanket around it so she could feed the hungry child. Once the bottle was set, she carefully maneuvered the car out of the shed and down the driveway to the main road. She glanced in the rearview mirror one last time at the colonial house where she'd lived and been employed for the past year. The clock on the dash showed it was just coming up on 8:00 p.m. It would be a little over an hour before she reached her parents' farm, where she'd grown up.

Emma was only twenty years old and still wasn't sure if she was ready to be a mother. She hoped her parents would know what to do.

CHAPTER 1

TWENTY-THREE YEARS LATER
GEORGIA

J ACQUI SLOWED HER BREATHING WHILE HOLDING THE closed switchblade between her lips. She was on her stomach, lying under a vehicle, and from her position, she could see a man approaching. The gravel crunched beneath his feet as he moved across the parking lot toward the vehicle. She was happy her intel was correct and there were only two guards on duty tonight. The crunching of the gravel got louder as the man rounded the rear of the SUV to get in through the driver's side. When his feet stopped beside the door, Jacqui reached out with her Kukri machete and sliced through the Achilles tendon on his right leg. She dropped the machete when the man crumpled to the ground, grunting, and before he could cry out in pain, she rolled out from under the SUV, clamped her left hand over his mouth, and sank the tip of her smaller blade into his medulla. She turned it ninety degrees clockwise and waited until he stopped moving. She pulled it out and rolled up to her feet, staying in a crouched position. Staring at the building, her eyes roamed over all the windows looking for anyone else, but she saw no other activity except for the mark still sitting at the table in the conference room upstairs.

She pivoted, moving to the other side of the man she'd just taken out. She wiped her blade off on his shirt and unzipped the front of her racing suit, tucking the small blade into a pocket of her tact vest before zipping it up. She slid the machete back into the sheath on her back.

Jacqui rolled the body under the SUV, remaining low while she made one last visual perimeter check with her monocular for anybody roaming around outside. It was clear. She knew there were only three people inside the building: the mark and two guards downstairs in the lobby. She was grateful she'd been able to sneak in late last night to set up her circuit interrupter, which tapped into the camera feed and hid her presence.

She tucked the monocular into the small backpack she was wearing, adjusted her balaclava, and moved quickly to the stairs on the side of the building. The second level offered a fire escape ladder attached to the side of the structure, making it easier to get to the rooftop. She climbed the ladder and moved to the center of the roof, where the skylight was located.

She peered down through the window at the mark, who was just finishing up a call. These late-night international video calls sure did come in handy for night jobs. She pulled the switchblade back out, and once the laptop was closed, she hit the corner of the skylight with the opposite end, shattering the glass, and dropped straight down onto the table. She pulled her PPK380 with the suppressor and shot him once in the face just under his nose and twice in the chest. His body slumped over in the chair. Job complete.

Jacqui tucked the weapons back inside her suit and zipped it up just as her watch buzzed with an incoming text. Good, the payment for her last job had just posted. She noted the time and sent a quick confirmation for the current job. She walked to the edge of the table, then squatted before dropping down to the floor.

She quietly moved toward the door and cracked it open to listen, picking up on the voices of the guards who had heard the noise upstairs and were on their way to check it out. She peeked down the empty hallway and stepped out, moving to the small closet she'd found when she reviewed the floor plan and other schematics for the building. She climbed up into the air duct, then inched her way through until she reached the electrical room. She pulled the tile back and dropped down to the floor, moving quickly over to the panel to remove the circuit interrupter installed the previous night. She tucked it inside her suit, climbed back up into the air duct, and continued to crawl to the opposite end of the hallway. She dropped out of the ceiling and into the closet and listened at the door. She heard voices in the distance and determined they were at the other end of the hall. They sounded calm—and then she heard raised voices. They'd found the body. *Time to go.*

Jacqui slowly and quietly opened the door, again listening to determine their exact location. Looking across the hallway, she smiled when she noticed the door to the stairs. It was always nice when the schematics matched reality. Moving across the hall and through the door, she raced down to the outside door and climbed down the ladder. She crouched behind a small wall and listened to see if the authorities had been notified yet. Only the everyday sounds of the city could be heard. She stood and vaulted the railing to the ground. She ran over and got on her bike, pulling on her helmet. She took one last glance at the building before starting the engine and driving off into the night.

Jacqui slowed the bike and turned off the main road onto a dirt driveway, then paused at the gate to check the perimeter on her watch. She loved her gadgets. All clear and no alerts. She entered a code into a box mounted just outside the gate. It opened, and she drove the bike down the long dirt driveway, rolling up to an old barn. She stopped the bike on a concrete slab to the left of the building and cut the engine, setting the stand in place. She got off, removed her helmet, and set it on the seat. She walked toward the building and pushed on the bottom edge of the siding. A small section sank in and slid down to reveal a panel. She removed her right glove and placed her hand on the glass, looking into a screen. Once the scan of her hand and retina were complete, the panel turned green and a mechanism for the lock could be heard through the door. She pushed the door all the way open and walked back to the bike, wheeling it into the structure. After opening another door on the left side of the hallway just a few feet from the one she came through, she put the bike away, staring at it a few moments. She grabbed a cheesecloth and gave it a quick wipe-down before finally putting the cover over it. There was something about the Ducati that had captured her heart from the moment she saw it. The first time she'd ridden one was unlike anything she'd ever experienced in her lifetime, all twenty-three years. She walked back over and closed the main door, locking it.

Happy to be home, she sighed, removing her balaclava. She grabbed a water from the refrigerator and ran upstairs to get cleaned up. She took a sip, pulling all the cameras up on her laptop, reviewing them as she unzipped her jacket and removed the tact vest. All weapons were laid out to be cleaned later; she was too damn hungry at the moment. She pulled up her favorite burger joint and placed an order to be picked up. She removed the rest of her body armor and clothing. She walked toward the bathroom and pinned her long braid on top of her head to take a quick shower.

Jacqui stepped out, appreciating the warm Georgia night as she dressed quickly in blue jeans and a royal-blue T-shirt, throwing on her leathers and her matching brown leather jacket. She quickly redid her braid, added some tinted lip balm to her lips, and grabbed her helmet. She didn't really wear makeup, just a good moisturizer and lip balm with some color. Being outside a lot gave her a nice natural glow and a sprinkle of freckles across her nose and cheeks. Her eyes popped all by themselves since they were a unique indigo color, and her auburn hair had its fair share of highlights strategically distributed because her hair was almost always in a side braid.

She locked everything up and got on her Harley Fat Boy and rode back into town to her favorite burger joint. Well, not really in town. She lived in Dickey, which was technically an unincorporated part of Calhoun County in Georgia, so running out to grab a burger or good food of any kind was more like a forty-five-minute ride. She didn't care. It gave her time to process the events of the day or think about how she would execute any new jobs coming up. Plus, it was a beautiful night for a ride.

Jacqui pulled into the parking lot and parked her bike away from other vehicles. She got off and walked toward the building, noting all the activity happening around her. These guys were always busy, and she understood why—the service was good and the food was even better.

Approaching the counter, she noticed it was the same kid who was usually working when she came in. He actually looked just a few years younger than she was but, considering what she did for a living, she knew their perceptions on life were very different—not to mention the fact that she'd traveled the world right after she turned seventeen.

"That was a double burger with pepper jack, red onions, and sauce, plus an order of fries to go, for Smith?"

His name was Brian, and like every other time she'd seen him, he was smiling like a fool.

"Yes," she confirmed.

She watched as he pulled her order from the back counter and carefully carried the large bag over to her.

He handed her the order and beamed at her like she was a goddess. "Please come again."

She chuckled, setting the cash down on the counter with a tip. "Thanks."

He was a nice kid and always gave her extra napkins and sauce, which was cool. No matter his reasoning, he really had the art of customer service down. He was cute, but she would never consider allowing anything to happen with him, no matter how long it had been for her. It just wasn't really her style. Besides, she wanted a man, someone who wouldn't be scared shitless when they learned what she did for a living.

Jacqui walked out of the restaurant and toward her bike, smiling to herself when the thought of Denner popped into her head. Now, *he* was a man, and she knew after doing a background check that he would be able to handle what she did for a living. *Hell*, she had a feeling he already knew a few things, what with the special projects he'd worked on with her for her vehicles. *Hmm, maybe . . .*

She stored the food in the side bag where she kept her saddlebag cooler, perfect for keeping things warm or cold for the long ride home. She climbed back onto her bike and pulled her helmet on, looking around one last time before turning the engine over. She flipped her face guard down, slowly maneuvering the bike across the back of the lot, when an older beat-up truck pulled in with its music blaring and cut her off. Her body jerked forward in the seat; she was glad she hadn't been going faster. A guy got out and smiled at her, making a bigger deal than necessary with his *bullshit* apology. She paused for a moment, staring in his direction.

"Sorry, *honey!*" He blew her a kiss and started laughing his ass off.

Jacqui steered her bike around his shitty truck, slowing down when she saw some loose rocks on the pavement. She aligned her fat rear tire over them perfectly before causing the tire to break and sending them flying like shrapnel behind her at the asshole. One hit him in the side of his right leg, causing him to yelp and swear, while three more hit his truck, including one cracking his windshield.

"You bitch!" he yelled.

She laughed, speeding off into the night, happy to get back to her peace and quiet.

Jacqui arrived home, riding down the dark driveway and stopping the bike in front of the center doors of the house. She cut the engine and dropped the stand, climbing off and then walking over to open the double doors. She pulled the bike inside what looked to be an old run-down barn, which was set in the middle of a piece of land far off the main road. With no immediate neighbors, it was perfect for someone who wasn't looking to be noticed, which offered her the privacy she wanted and needed.

Her home was not what it seemed, since it was actually made up of six forty-foot-long shipping containers, including two underground that served as additional storage and a shooting range. There were two levels aboveground, and then the entire structure was made to look like an old barn. She'd decided to use two twenty footers that sat perpendicular against the end of the forties in front, which offered even more storage, like a pantry. Inside, she had stacked bales of straw along the outer walls for extra insulation and protection from bullets. A girl in her line of work could never be too careful.

She parked the bike and set her helmet on a shelf above it before removing the bag with her dinner from the saddle-bag. The smell made her stomach growl, and she laughed to herself. As she crossed the center of the structure, the straw on the floor crunched under her boots. She punched a code in and entered on the west side through the living room, setting her dinner down on the coffee table. She ran upstairs and opened her laptop, quickly checking the cameras and the dark web to see if any interesting new jobs had come across the wire. *Hmm, nothing great. Maybe something will pop up tomorrow morning.*

Then again, she needed to check on the status of her new truck. She chuckled, thinking about seeing *him* tomorrow.

She closed the laptop and went back downstairs to eat and relax, pleased when she found a movie to watch on Netflix.

CHAPTER 2

J ACQUI AWOKE WITH A START, FEELING CONFUSED AND AN-gry until she realized it had just been a dream. Not really a dream, but the memory of when she was a little girl and found the photo album. She lay in bed, staring up at the ceiling, remembering when she'd run into the kitchen and confronted Emma, demanding to know who the people in the photos were. That was when she'd learned the truth about who she was and what had happened to her real parents.

Emma had confessed that she was really the nanny whom her mother had hired and then entrusted to save her only child. It was overwhelming to hear when she was only nine years old, and she hadn't taken it well. Emma had tried to explain the reasons her mother had given her up, telling Jacqui about conversations she'd overheard between her mother and father while she was employed with them. Jacqui had known for years the information Emma had shared with her was not complete, and she'd always wondered if she would ever have all the answers.

Savannah DeMott, Jacqui's mother, was very pregnant and due at any time. Her husband, Victor, was worried about her stress level and the baby, and he was determined not to allow the merger his brother-in-law was pushing to go through. The reputation of the company they had started together was far more important than a pile of money. Lionel, his brother-in-law, didn't seem to get that. It had taken a couple of years for Victor to realize going into business with him had been a huge mistake. Victor had been diligently working in secret, trying to complete a deal that would allow him to offer to buy Lionel out. The man had become very aggressive with his intentions, and now Victor feared for his wife and unborn child. He had no doubt Lionel would get rid of anyone who got in his way, including his own blood relatives.

Jacqui glanced at the clock on her nightstand and rolled her eyes: 5:45 a.m. *Close enough*. She had a lot to do, so the early start was just a bonus. She reached over and slid the switch for the alarm to off before sitting up and swinging her legs over the side of her bed. The sun wouldn't be up for another hour and a half, which was fine. She reached for the lamp and flipped the light on, pulling the photo album from the shelf. She opened it to the middle to the images of her parent's wedding; they were so young and happy. Her focus lingered on the gentleman standing next to her father. They were both laughing. She smirked, wondering why she'd never noticed him before as she pulled the picture out and turned it over. Anderson Steele. She looked at the picture again, and this time she noticed a man in the background staring at the happy couple with a slight grimace on his face. She wondered . . .

One thing she did know was that she needed to clear her head, and nothing did that like a killer workout.

Jacqui put the picture back and closed the album, then placed it back on the shelf. She looked around her bedroom, taking in the workspace she had set up and the hardwood floors that had been installed throughout the living space. There were area rugs under the heavier pieces of furniture, which also helped define the different spaces; at least, that's what the designer had told her was the decision behind her purchases. It was the same contemporary design and hardwood floors that had been installed downstairs. Everything was functional, without fuss. She dealt with enough fuss in her professional life—no need to have it at home too. She glanced up at the vaulted ceiling she and the architect had created together by removing the tops from the upper containers, which allowed for a higher ceiling and windows to be installed in the angled roof. She'd also had a ladder mounted on the wall, allowing her to climb up to the roof if she wanted, and there was a ledge next to the ladder where she stored certain items. All in all, she'd been very happy with how her house had turned out.

She stood and walked over to grab her telescoping pole off the wall to open the windows wider in the roofline, hoping to catch a breeze or two when they came through the area. It also helped that she usually slept in the nude. Even with the windows open, it could get too hot and muggy. She slid the double barn doors open that looked out below to the front of the barn before walking into the bathroom. She washed her face and brushed her teeth, then quickly put on her workout clothes. She wanted to knock it out and then drive out to the farm where she'd grown up to see Emma and her family. A pang of guilt settled in her stomach for a moment when she realized how long it had been since she'd visited them. They always seemed to understand, yet Jacqui suddenly felt inclined to do better and visit them more frequently. She was also hoping to see Pham Long, to talk about her memories and what she felt it was time to do. She owed him so much. *Hell*, she owed all of them. Pham Long had been born in Vietnam and moved to the United States after his wife and daughter were killed in an accident. The details of the accident were not known, and he'd never offered to explain things. He'd worked on the Daniels' farm for many years before Jacqui arrived, but he'd always seemed mysterious and a little spooky to her when she was younger. Then one day, everything changed and they became fast friends. He'd decided to share with her Vovinam, the Vietnamese martial arts he'd learned as a child. Soon he'd become Chu Long to Jacqui, teaching her how to control her anger and frustration and how to channel it in a way that benefited her and didn't hurt others. Before he'd started training her, there had been several random fights at school and nobody wanted to be her friend, leaving her feeling even more isolated. This had only made a bad situation worse. She still practiced Vovinam because it had served her well.

Growing up on a farm had given her several advantages for lifting and maneuvering heavy things like bales of straw or buckets of feed. Now she used those components as part of her training—bales of straw for squats and buckets of feed or rocks for lunges and curls. Plus, climbing a rope from the ground to the ceiling was always great for building up endurance and overall strength. She made more than enough money to go out and buy the correct weight sets or whatever, but she preferred to remind herself daily what she'd survived and where she'd come from.

Just as she reached the top of the rope for the last time, she heard the phone ring and then her fax line. Maybe a new job was coming in. But first, breakfast.

Jacqui climbed back down the rope and studied her gloves when she hit the ground. The warmth of the leather made her smile as she pulled the gloves off and tossed them in the bucket against the wall. She walked through the pantry into the kitchen to wash her hands and splash water on her face. She ran her wet hands over her shoulders and down her arms a few times to cool down, wiping her hands off on her sweats. She reached for her phone and checked her voicemail, hitting the speakerphone button so she could listen while she pulled a steak and eggs from the refrigerator.

"Jacqui, it's Denner. I'm still workin' on your new truck, but I had a few cost differences pop up. I sent you a fax. Let me know what you wanna do."

She saved the message and got back to making her breakfast, pushing the button to start brewing the coffee. She placed a steak in a large pan and tossed in a couple of eggs to scramble at the same time. The cost of getting what she needed and what she wanted for her work truck was never going to be an issue, but she appreciated his call.

Finn "Denner" Dennis was the best tech in town, and there didn't seem to be anything he couldn't build or fix. She'd found him when she first moved into the area and performed a background check on him, like she did with most people she chose to work with. She'd been thrilled when he passed with flying colors, having served eight years in the army as a Ranger, and now he owned his own shop. He was also sexy as hell. Jacqui never wanted him to know how she felt—although she often wondered if he already *did* know. It would certainly explain why he was always asking her out, not in a *gross* way or like some *assholes* she'd encountered. Just politely persistent.

She smiled to herself as she flipped her steak, searing the opposite side and pulling the eggs out onto a plate.

Her thoughts went back to Denner, with his dark hair and beard, his ruggedly handsome face, and warm brown eyes that just pulled you in. Not to mention his six-foot-three-inch frame, which probably weighed in at around two twenty-five, and the many tattoos etched down those tanned, muscular arms.

Damn! Okay, J, stop thinking about the hot man and focus on your steak.

She pulled it from the pan and set it on the plate next to her eggs. Coffee was done, so she added heavy creamer to a large mug and topped it off with the fresh brew.

She carried everything over to the bar top on her island and dug in as her mind wandered back to Denner. There was just something about *him*. He seemed naturally understanding, like a live-and-let-live kinda guy, and when she allowed it, he made her laugh. She just liked keeping everything on a business level where he was concerned, doing her best not to encourage him. When he'd learned what she did for a living, he expressed concern for her well-being. She'd told him not to worry but ultimately knew he would ignore her request. He'd told her once if she ever got in trouble to give him a call. So far, that day had never come.

She finished her breakfast and put her dishes in the dishwasher before heading upstairs to review the fax he'd sent over. It wasn't too bad. A few parts were more and others were less, producing around a fifty-dollar difference on the higher side. She appreciated his honesty, though. Some places would've just done the work and not given you a heads-up. *Damn!* Another one of his great qualities. She'd stop by on her way back into town. For now, she needed a shower. *Probably a cold one.*

She pulled off her workout clothes and tossed them into the dirty bin. She was walking toward the bathroom but changed her direction when another fax came through. She looked over the paper. It was a job in New Orleans, one she'd actually been waiting for. The mark was a regular at one of the local "houses"—a standing appointment, so to speak. She confirmed the job with a fax reply. Judging by the time, she'd have to leave extra early the morning of that job. She also did a search for Anderson Steele, locating him rather quickly. She loaded his address into her phone and moved toward the bathroom to get cleaned up.

CHAPTER 3

J ACQUI ARRIVED AT THE FARM A FEW HOURS LATER. SHE parked her Harley over by the barn, backing it into position before turning off the engine. She unsnapped her helmet and removed it, setting it on the front of the bike. Everything looked the same for the most part, except many of the trees in the orchard were much taller now; she could see the workers collecting the peaches. She laughed, looking at the peanut field on the opposite side of the property, when a fond memory popped into her head. Her first time collecting that crop earned her some teasing.

"Jacqueline!" a woman's voice called out, coming toward her.

Jacqui turned her head, smiled, and waved, getting off her bike. It wasn't just any woman—it was the woman who'd raised her.

Jacqui chuckled when she saw Copper and Rusty, the Australian shepherds, racing toward her, barking and carrying on when they recognized her. Emma had handpicked them from a litter when they were just puppies and had trained them well. Jacqui bent down to greet them, laughing as they both nuzzled and licked her face, pressing their bodies into her.

"It's been too long." Emma paused, studying Jacqui. "Been working a lot?"

"Oh yeah." Jacqui stood and embraced her. "How are you, Em?"

"I'm good." Emma smiled, studying her as she took her jacket off and turned it inside out before laying it across the seat.

"I've just been busy." Jacqui glanced down the long driveway, avoiding eye contact.

"You had another dream, didn't you?"

"What makes you ask?" Jacqui looked back at Emma and then down, kicking some of the smaller rocks with the toe of her boot.

"Because you look a little tired. Good, but tired."

Emma reached over and brushed a stray auburn hair off her adopted daughter's sun-kissed face.

Jacqui sighed, wrapping her arms around the woman, holding her in a long embrace. "Sorry it's been so long."

"It's okay, sweetie." Emma pulled back and looked at her. "I know your life is nothing like what your parents had planned, but I tried to make it the best I could for you."

They started walking up the driveway toward the house.

"I know, and thank you." Jacqui chuckled. "It wasn't your fault the clay you had to work with was so resistant to being molded."

Emma laughed. "Wow! That was philosophical. Been doing a lot of reading lately?"

"No." Jacqui giggled. "I think I'm just preparing for my conversation with him. It's been a while since we've *really* talked."

"I understand. You know, I think he's really missed your talks over the years, and missed training with you," Emma declared.

"Really? What makes you say that?"

"Because he started teaching me some Vovinam the last year or so." Emma chuckled. "It's good stuff."

"Ever had to use it?"

"Thankfully, not yet." They stopped, and Emma turned to face her again. "Well, he's over in the shed. I know he'd love to see you."

"Thanks." Jacqui turned and started walking away from her.

"Hey, don't leave without coming into the house. I know Mom and Dad would love to see you too."

"I will. I promise." Jacqui walked toward the shed, thinking about her grandparents, Keith and Carol Daniels. They were two of the most generous and kindest people she'd ever met, and she was grateful to have them in her life.

Emma watched as Jacqui strolled across the driveway, heading around the corner from the main house. Emma had never married and now, at forty-four, she didn't think she ever would. It wasn't because she thought she was too old. For her, making the promise she'd made to Savannah DeMott meant she was determined to spend her life always being there for Jacqueline, for whatever she needed. It just seemed like the right thing to do.

Jacqui thought about the man she was on her way to speak to, the one who'd saved her in ways no one else could've. She smirked to herself, remembering how hurt and angry she'd been when she found the bag with the family photo album inside, along with the note her birth mother had given to Emma. It was a lot for a nine-year-old to discover and deal with, and Jacqui had read the note so many times that she'd memorized it.

> *Sweet Emma,*
>
> *Please keep my daughter safe and raise her as if she were your own. I know if she stays, they will kill her too. They must never know she survived, or they will come looking for her.*
>
> *The holding shares in her father's company would make her CEO, and her father and I knew that would never be allowed. There is money in the bag and more in the trunk of the car, to help you take care of her and for her future.*
>
> *The photo album is for you to share with her when she's old enough to learn the truth. I know you will do right by her, which is why I'm trusting you with the most precious thing in my life, my precious baby girl, Jacqueline Indigo DeMott.*
>
> *Savannah DeMott*

Little Jacqueline had been so angry, storming into the kitchen where Emma and Carol were making dinner. She'd thrown the photo album at Emma, screaming at her.

"Why did you lie to me? You're not my real mom!" Tears streamed down her face, and her little hands were balled into fists.

"Jacqueline, please." Emma walked over to her, crouching to look her in the eye. "Please let me explain."

"No!" She raised her arms like she might hit Emma. Instead, she dropped them to her sides, repeatedly hitting the sides of her little legs. "Tell me what happened to my parents. Why didn't they want me?"

"Jacqueline, sweetie, it's going to be okay," her grandmother declared.

Jacqui's eyes never left Emma's face.

"Oh, Jacqueline, baby I'm so sorry you found out this way." Emma's soothing tone was not enough.

There were just too many questions a nine-year-old should never have to ask. She reached out, but the child pulled back.

"No, leave me alone! I hate you!"

Jacqui had run out of the house and didn't stop until she'd reached the small pond on the property. She'd stood at the edge of the water, crying, and when a family of ducks appeared, she picked up some rocks and began throwing them as hard as she could, trying to hit them. When she was unsuccessful and out of rocks, she fell to her knees, sobbing hysterically, crying so hard that she never even heard Mr. Long's footsteps.

He sat down near her and patiently waited for her to catch her breath and stop crying.

"It will be okay, *tre em*. I can help you with your anger and sadness."

"You don't know what I'm feeling." She pulled her little legs into her chest, hugging them to feel safe.

"Oh, but I do." He paused. "You see, I too have lost someone dear to me, and I understand more than you know how much it hurts."

She looked over at him, and he could tell she was trying to decide if she should trust him.

"I can help you channel your anger and frustration." He saw doubt behind her eyes. "If nothing else, I can teach you how to throw a rock correctly."

A small smile tugged at the sides of her mouth. "Yeah?"

"Oh yes—but if I teach you, you must promise me you will never throw rocks at ducks again."

"Okay. I didn't really want to hit them. I just wanted to hit *something*." Her eyes cast down at the ground after her confession.

"And I will teach you how to hit and when. Do we have a deal?" He extended his arm to shake her hand.

She shifted her body to face him and smiled, pressing her small hand into his. "Deal." Then her little face turned dark, and she pulled her hand back, hugging her knees to her chest again.

"*Tre em?* Tell me what happened."

Jacqueline looked out across the pond, watching the family of ducks all swimming together.

"Those people in the house are not my family. Turns out, my parents just gave me away, like they didn't want me." New tears rolled down her cheeks.

He moved closer to her, pulling her little body into his. "Is that what you were told?"

"No, but I found the note."

"Perhaps there is more to learn and understand than what was simply written in a note." He sighed. "*Tre em*, you should allow Miss Emma to tell you what happened. It will not be easy for you to hear; however, I believe then you will have a better understanding."

She looked up into his face, her beautiful indigo eyes framed in redness. "I'm scared."

"I know. The unknown can be a scary thing." He paused. "Have they not always taken care of you and loved you for who you are?"

"Yes."

"Then honor that by giving them the opportunity to explain the circumstances of how you came to be with them. Can you do that, *tre em*?"

She nodded, resting her head against his chest.

"Good."

Jacqui smiled at the memory, rounding the corner of the shed. She knocked but there was no answer. Then she heard his voice.

"Hello, *tre em*. Come, please."

She turned, beaming, when she saw him sitting in a small clearing just past the tall grass. He was working on a new basket.

He was only around five feet, six inches tall, and his hair had always had sprinkles of gray in it, although now there was more. His eyes danced with a mixture of wisdom and mischief, and he had a laugh that warmed your heart.

"Care to join me in a project?"

"I would love to, thank you."

Jacqui took a seat next to him, looking over at the basket he'd been working on. "It's coming along nicely."

"Yes." He nodded. "It should be done by end of day."

She reached over and collected two different colors to start her own basket. They worked in silence for about forty-five minutes, enjoying each other's company and the warmth of the sun shining down on their faces.

"I see you have kept your fingers strong and nimble over the years." He chuckled. "Must be from all that *private secu-rity* work you do."

"What do you mean?" She looked at him.

He stopped weaving and rolled his eyes. "*Tre em*, I *know*."

"You know *what*?" Her coyness as she focused on her checkered pattern made him chuckle again.

"I know you feel like you must live in the dark and the light. That is why you always liked the plaiting when you weave. Never one color, always a balance between dark and light." He looked at her and smirked. "Such is your life."

"Okay, but it's lookin' good, right?" She held up her project to show her progress.

"Hmm, good thing you have more time, because it needs more work." He chuckled. "Tell me about the dream."

Jacqui sighed, staring up at the sky. "It was like some of the others, and then it wasn't."

"Meaning?"

"Well, there was the photo album I found that told me the truth about my parents and the conversation Emma had with me explaining how they were killed. Then I woke up."

"How did you feel when you awoke?"

"Angry." She paused. "I pulled the album off the shelf and started looking through it again. I've looked through it so many times, but this time I couldn't take my eyes off a man in a few of the wedding pictures. I pulled one of the pictures out and found his name on the back. He was a lawyer and the best man. I found his house, so I'm going to go speak with him. Maybe he can fill in some of the blanks. Of course, I also kept looking at the other man in several of the photos—the one who took my parents from me."

"And what did you decide?"

"I believe it's time I introduced myself." She shook her head. "After all this time, it's still hard for me to believe a member of my family wanted me dead, only days after I came into this world."

"I think it's time for you to go get your duck." He looked at her and winked.

She laughed at his reference to their shared memory. "I don't plan to miss this time." She kept weaving.

"I know you won't. Being a bounty hunter has been very lucrative for you." He chuckled when her jaw dropped. "I like your style."

"How did you know? Does anybody else know?" She looked over her shoulder in the direction of the house. "They can't ever find out; it will put them in danger."

"Relax, *tre em*. I am the only one who knows, and I will never tell." He continued weaving his basket.

"How is it *you* know?"

"I have people."

"*You* have people?" Her body shifted toward him. "Does this have anything to do with your life in Vietnam?"

He stopped weaving and gazed out across the tall green grass around them. "When I think of my homeland, I prefer to think of beautiful things, like Phong Nha-Ke Bang National Park. The ancient caves, underground rivers, and turquoise lakes are simply stunning to see. I don't think about the reason I left." He resumed his project. "I would really like to see the Golden Bridge someday."

"It's quite stunning in its own right. Maybe we can see it together." Jacqui looked back over at him. "You must be disappointed in me." She hung her head, resting her project in her lap.

"On the contrary." He stopped and looked at her. "I believe you to be incredibly brave and resourceful. You took a horrible and quite possibly very damaging beginning to your life and became someone others could depend on, to right wrongs and bring justice to their plights."

"Wow, I never heard of a bounty hunter or mercenary's actions described quite like that before. So poetic," she teased him. "Thank you. Wait, how was I resourceful?"

"Oh, Miss Jacqueline, do you believe I ever thought you were just *bumming* around Europe for all those years?" He chuckled and shook his head. "No, no. You took the fundamentals of Vovinam I taught you and then elevated your knowledge and *skill* set. I imagine there are many more techniques you've learned over the years."

"Well, I *was* actually traveling to several different countries, so at least that part was true," she sheepishly confirmed.

"I understand—and yes, *that* part *was* true."

"Thank you, Chu Long. I feel like a weight has been lifted." She set her project aside and stood.

"Where are you going, *tre em*? You have not finished your basket."

"I will come back another day to finish. For now, I need to go see my grandparents, and then I've got work to do." She winked.

He nodded and watched as she walked away. That duck had no idea what was coming.

TWO HOURS LATER, JACQUI GOT ON HER BIKE AND STARTED the engine, understanding now why she'd had the dream again. Seeing her grandparents was always a great reminder of how far she'd come. Chu Long had been right all those years ago when he'd reminded her of their patience and acceptance of her, considering how angry and troubled she'd been. There was no way she would allow any harm to come to them. She needed to go see that lawyer. Hopefully, he would be home. She also needed to go see Denner about her new truck, and then it was time she figured out how she was going to deal with the duck.

CHAPTER 4

A N HOUR LATER, JACQUI PULLED UP TO A TUDOR-STYLE house in the quiet neighborhood of Johns Creek, cutting the engine on her motorcycle. She glanced around, wondering how many motorcycles had ever been in this area before and actually stopped instead of just passing through. Not that it mattered. There was a man she needed to see.

She removed her helmet and pulled her phone from the inside pocket of her jacket, double-checking the address, which was a match to the house she was sitting in front of. She sighed, climbing off the bike, wondering how this would go.

According to her findings, the man was married with a couple of kids—not that she figured they'd be home. They were most likely off at college or at work. She hadn't bothered to dig that far.

She walked up to the door and rang the bell, desperately trying to slow her heart rate while she waited. It was ridiculous to her that she could face off with assholes and creeps but meeting an old friend of her father's, the father she'd never known, was *terrifying*.

A beautiful woman with golden bronzed skin opened the door, smiling. "Can I help you?" She was elegantly dressed in casual clothing, and her makeup was immaculate.

"Yes, I'm looking for Anderson Steele." Jacqui focused on the helmet under her arm to calm herself.

"Honey, who is it?" a man's voice on the other side of the door asked.

"It's a young woman—I'm sorry, dear, what was your name?" the woman asked.

"My name is—"

The door opened wider, and a handsome middle-aged Black man who resembled a fine country gentleman peered around the edge of it. His eyes widened, and his mouth curled into a surprised smile.

"Well, I'll be *damned*." He stared at Jacqui for a moment and then turned to his wife. "Honey, can you make us some of that fine sweet tea of yours and bring it to the study?" He looked back at Jacqui. "We have a lot to talk about."

"Certainly." She smiled and kissed him on the cheek.

"Please, come in," Anderson offered.

Jacqui wiped her feet before walking into one of the most beautiful homes she'd ever seen in real life.

"I'm sorry if I'm intruding on your time, Mr. Steele." She looked around nervously, her eyes taking in the black-and-white pattern on the floor and the antique-looking table in the middle of the entryway. There was a formal dining room off to the left of the entryway and a beautiful living room on the right. Suddenly, she felt incredibly out of place.

"Nonsense." His eyes shone as he looked at her. "I've been expecting you for a while now. Let's go into my study."

She nodded and followed him through the elegant living room decorated in neutral tones with softly painted walls and sparsely hung artwork. The area rug absorbed the sounds of their shoes as they moved past the main sitting area and into a room on the back side of the house. There was a large mahogany desk across the room, a fireplace with matching mahogany around the edge and mantel, and a wall of built-in floor-to-ceiling bookcases.

He closed the door behind them, and she turned to face him.

"I can't believe you're here," he whispered, staring at her. "Jacqueline Indigo DeMott. You *are* a perfect blend of your parents." He gestured to a chair across from the desk. "Please."

"Thank you."

She stepped away from him and took a seat, wondering if she'd made a mistake.

Anderson took a seat behind his desk and chuckled. "I'm sorry for staring. I know you have questions, and I want to help you any way I can."

"Thank you, Mr. Steele. I appreciate that." She set her helmet on the floor. "I guess my first question is, how well did you know my father? I mean, I know you were the best man at his wedding, but how long had you been friends?"

"Your father and I had been friends since college. He was studying for the business world, and I was gearing up to make the grade to get into law school, but we stayed in touch even after we graduated."

"What was he like?"

"Your dad was one hell of an athlete and smart as a whip." He chuckled, leaning back in his chair, remembering something fond from the past. "Victor was always proving people wrong, especially when they thought he was just a dumb jock." He laughed softly again. "In fact, that's how he won your mother."

She smiled. "What do you mean, 'won' her?"

"Well, your mother was at a basketball game with her friend who attended the rival school. When she caught your daddy's eye, Victor decided right then and there he was gonna marry that girl." He paused, his face reflecting on times gone by. "Ooh, your mother was a real beauty, with her soft, red hair and bright-blue eyes."

"And what did my mother think of him?"

"Well, she was intrigued, but she wasn't going to make it easy for him. The fact she didn't attend either school drove him crazy, trying to figure out where she came from. And of course, asking her friend was not possible, since she attended the rival school and he had no idea who she was either. All he got from your mother that night was her name. So naturally, Victor worked harder to impress her by tracking her down." He leaned forward. "You know, we thought he was gonna have to take out a loan the first time he bought her flowers."

She giggled. "Why?"

"Because the man did his *damnedest* to purchase every white gardenia in the state of Georgia once he learned they were her favorite." He crossed his hands on his desk. "And that is how he won Miss Savannah Whitlock. From that moment on, they were inseparable."

Jacqui sat for a moment in silence, reflecting on everything she'd just heard.

"Thank you for sharing that with me. It helps a little, knowing how happy they were at one time." She looked across the desk, and she knew the look in her eyes had changed when his demeanor did too. "I know my father and uncle were in business together. What can you tell me about it?"

Anderson nodded and sat back in his chair again. His brow furrowed and a troubled look came over his face. "Your father and his brother-in-law, Lionel Whitlock, created a company together, DeWhit Holdings, offering consulting and investment services."

"So what happened?"

There was a knock at the door and it opened. "Sorry about interrupting, but I've got that tea for you all."

"Thank you, darlin'."

Mrs. Steele set the tray on his desk before smiling and leaving.

Anderson handed a glass to Jacqui and took the other for himself.

"Your father was doing quite well, and everything was great until Lionel started leaning on him to merge their company with another conglomerate—only Victor wanted nothing to do with them. Apparently, the company had done some questionable dealings in the past, and Victor really wanted to maintain a clean, professional view in the world."

"So, my father would talk with you about these things?"

"Absolutely. Victor and I always had each other's backs—like I said, even after we graduated. I would often help him with private legal matters, things he didn't want anyone other than your mother to know about." He paused and sadness washed over him. "When I'd heard he and Savannah had been murdered, I knew beyond a shadow of a doubt who was behind it. I was also not a bit surprised when your father's company merged with another."

"Why didn't you say anything?" Jacqui leaned forward, suddenly feeling frustrated. How could this man have remained silent?

Anderson looked at her, sorrow filling his chest. "Because I knew, according to the law, there was no way I could prove it, despite the fact I knew Lionel had said something to him that shook him to his core. It would have been considered hearsay."

"What threat did he make?"

"Victor never told me the details, he just came to me one day and had me start creating a secret portfolio and offshore accounts under your initials, JID." He set his tea down on the desk. "Whatever was said, your father feared for your well-being. Your mother was about seven and a half months pregnant when we got everything set up for you. We also contacted an older friend of ours in the medical community, who, after hearing about the situation, agreed to forge documents saying you died just after being born."

Jacqui felt like all the air had been suddenly sucked out of the room. She took a sip of her tea, trying to calm her nerves.

"That is how concerned your father was about whatever threat your uncle had made."

"Wasn't the doctor concerned about losing his medical license or going to jail?"

"Probably, but he wanted to help. He was older and close

to retirement age, so he just retired sooner than planned." He picked up his tea. "I believe he moved out of the country shortly after that."

Jacqui took a long sip of her tea and then set the glass on the desk. She stood and walked across the room, becoming angrier at the *shitty* reason her parents had been taken from this world, and from her. She turned and walked back over to her chair. She sat and exhaled.

"This offshore account, it still exists?"

"It does." He looked puzzled. "I have often tried to look you up but never found you."

Jacqui smirked. "My nanny, Emma, raised me. Apparently, my mother told her to keep me safe, so she took me back to her family's farm, far away from the city. She legally adopted me, giving me the name Jacqueline Daniels. It kept me safe, but then when I was nine, I found the photo album my mother had put together, and Emma filled in the blanks. I was devastated. I started getting in fights and becoming a real problem. One of the workers on the farm helped me channel my pain and anger. He taught me discipline and how to take care of myself.

"When I was seventeen I left the country, looking for more knowledge about various things." She paused. "Before I returned to the States, I changed my name to Jacqui Bleu and purchased a shelf company. Whenever I get hired for a job, it's under the name J. Bleu, which I'd found to be more lucrative if they don't know if they're hiring a man or a woman. It was the best way I found to avoid any preconceived notions."

"A shelf company, huh?" He chuckled, leaning back in his chair. "And what is it you do for a living?"

"I'm a bounty hunter. I also do *specialty* jobs under the name BJ Lock." She stared at him, surprised to see him so calm.

"I see." Anderson grinned. "Then I would say *that* man is in a whole heap of trouble."

"So, you'll help me?"

"I will, although I'm not too sure what I can help with, unless you've got something legal that needs to be filed."

"I'm thinking you might be able to help me with research, things I might not think to look into or perhaps how to gain controlling shares in the company to reverse the merger."

"I'm not sure a reversal would be possible after twenty-three years of solid business." He leaned back, shaking his head. "Even if some of the deals to make the company what it is today were a bit *shady*."

"Then I guess I'll go with Plan A." Jacqui's smile filled in the blanks.

He nodded in silence. "You know, I'm not a violent man, but that *son of a bitch* took my best friend and his lovely wife—so at this point, I will help you any way I can, in full support of Plan A."

Anderson stood, moving away from his desk and across the room to a painting on the wall. He pulled the right side of the frame toward him and opened a safe behind it. He removed two large envelopes and closed everything back up. He walked back over and took a seat.

"Here is all the information you need." He handed one of the envelopes to her.

She opened it and removed a bunch of papers, one of which was her original birth certificate.

"You should have no issues accessing the offshore account or any of the shareholding you have in the company."

"What about the certificate stating I died just after my birth?"

"They'll just chalk it up to a clerical error." He chuckled, watching her smile.

"Guess that makes two offshore accounts I have now."

She flipped the top sheet over and found the last will and testament for Victor DeMott. She didn't even bother trying to hide the few tears shed when she read her father's name at the top. She ran her fingertips over the print, swallowing hard.

"Unfortunately, since you only have four years to contest a will in Georgia after it's filed, not much can come of this. I'm sorry, Jacqui."

"I understand."

"I also have this." Anderson handed the second large envelope to her. "It contains information specifically about the partnership of DeWhit Holdings and the history of mergers and suggested mergers from Lionel. Victor and I had several private meetings about his concerns and the direction Lionel wanted to take their company. I'd advised him of the possible legal ramifications on all the so-called 'deals' Lionel was looking to pursue. A few of them might have yielded additional profits for the shareholders, but Victor was more concerned about the company's name and reputation, whereas Lionel was always just looking to make more money. He really didn't give a damn about the shareholders." He paused, giving her a moment to process everything. "There's also information regarding your father's instructions for me to start the process to buy Lionel out, essentially forcing him out of the company.

Sadly, he was killed before the process was completed, but that didn't stop me from keeping an eye on the company's activities for all these years."

She looked across at him and managed a smile. "Thank you. I appreciate all the information you've given me today. It *does* help."

"You *are* your father's daughter, and you have your mother's beauty." Anderson stood and extended his arm across to her. "It was a pleasure to meet you, my dear. Let me know if you need my assistance for anything, okay?"

She shook his hand, nodding while she watched his eyes. "Thanks. And thank you for helping my father look out for me."

"Please be careful, Jacqui. I don't want anything to happen to you. I have a feeling this world is more interesting with you in it." He stepped out from behind the desk. "I'll walk you out."

Anderson walked her to the door, and they said goodbye. Naturally, he was concerned about her safety, although he knew he really had no reason to be. This girl was smart, and in her line of work, he was confident she knew how to take care of herself.

CHAPTER 5

J ACQUI PARKED HER BIKE AND GOT OFF, LEAVING THE helmet on the seat. She had been riding all day, and for hours at a time. She shook her legs out a bit as she walked past a few cars on the property that looked like they could be used only for parts. She chuckled to herself. That's why she'd decided to work with Denner. He seemed to be a bit of a visionary when it came to creative solutions, and in her line of work, that was exactly what she needed.

She walked into the building, unzipping her jacket slightly to remove a folded piece of paper. Her heart skipped a beat when Denner walked through the door from the shop.

"Hey, Jacqui. You got my message?"

"I did. Thanks for givin' me a heads-up on the price differences." She studied his physique while his back was turned. His strong body was screaming at her today.

Another man wandered in from the shop, grinning as he approached the desk. "Hey, Jacqui."

"Hey, George. What's up?" She smiled.

"One guess." George grinned at Denner, quickly regretting it.

"Is that transmission job done yet?" Denner asked as he walked over to the corner desk.

"Um, no. I'll go finish that up. Good seeing you, Jacqui."

"You, too, George." She chuckled under her breath as he headed back into the shop.

Denner picked up a few pieces of paper off his desk, and when he turned suddenly, he grinned, noticing her eyes roaming over his body.

"Question?" His mischievous smile made her blush.

"Nope, not at all." She smirked to recover. "Hey, I know it will take a couple more days, but I was wondering if you can add this to the truck bed." She handed him the paper from her jacket. "I found this on Amazon."

He studied the image on the paper. "A bed slide organizer?" He looked at her. "Really?"

"Yes. It will make it easier to remove heavier items from the back; plus, I need to have the option of securing things." She pointed to the sturdy metal rails on the side and the eye loops.

He winked. "What the hell are you picking up?"

"Various things." She unzipped her jacket farther and pulled out her wallet. "Can I just pay now? I'm going to be unavailable for a day or two."

"Sure, but I'm going to see if I can get you a better deal on that slide." He took her card.

"Go ahead and just charge me, and we can work out the difference later."

"Okay." He smiled and punched the total in on his card machine before slipping the card into the end to complete the transaction. The reader beeped, and he handed the card back to her.

"Thanks."

He stapled all her receipts together and handed them to her, watching as she folded them neatly before tucking them inside her jacket.

"Thank you. Hey, I was wondering: How would you feel about finding me a buyer for my old truck and I'll give you twenty percent of the sale."

"Yeah, I can do that. Thanks."

He looked deep into those indigo eyes, smiling when they dilated more. Her dark-auburn hair was secured on the left in a long braid, and her long lashes added more than enough color to her sun-kissed face. Her full lips were the perfect shade of burgundy rose.

Too many nights, he'd thought about those lips. He'd never seen her with her hair down—or with makeup on, for that matter. Not that she needed it. Her natural beauty and confidence were captivating.

"So, where are you headed?" he asked.

"Out of town on business." She zipped up her jacket. "I'll come by when I get back." She was out the door before he could ask any more questions. *That was close.*

She picked up her pace, trying to put more distance between them. *Damn*, that man was fine, but business was business and that's how it needed to stay. No time for romantic entanglements. She'd *had* romance in her life before. While she was traveling the world, she'd dated a few guys here and there. Mostly military. They knew things nobody else could teach her; plus, she didn't seem to scare the hell out of them, so bonus. Military guys were who she was usually drawn to, which explained her attraction to Denner. That, and he was *hot as hell.*

Her stomach growled. She pulled out her phone and called one of her favorite places, ordering a steak and potato to go. She ended the call and was surprised when she saw Denner's feet next to hers.

"Hey, I located that slider at a better price." He handed her a receipt. "This is for the difference."

"Thanks."

"Sorry, I didn't mean to interrupt your call." He smiled at her.

"You're not interrupting. I was just ordering some dinner to pick up on the way home." She folded the paper and tucked it away.

"Or you could let *me* take you to dinner."

"We've talked about this."

"Not really. I ask you out, and you always say no."

She picked up her helmet and swung her leg over her bike. "Sounds like a conversation to me." She put her helmet on.

He laughed. "Harley Fat Boy, right?"

"Yeah."

"It suits you."

"Does it?" She was intrigued.

"Yeah, it matches your *don't give a fuck* attitude." He crossed his arms over his chest, smiling at her.

"Funny, that's exactly what the salesman told me." She secured her chinstrap and shrugged.

He laughed, shaking his head. "Okay, I'll call you in a couple of days to let you know when the truck is done."

"Thanks." She started her bike and watched as he slowly backed away.

Yep, that was one hot man. Guess she'd have to settle for the vibrations of the bike tonight.

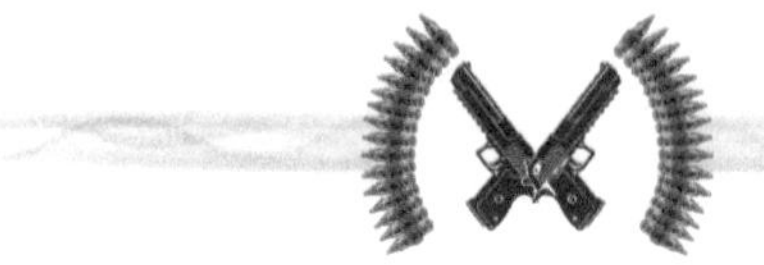

Jacqui arrived home with food and Denner still on her mind. It never ceased to amaze her how hungry she got from riding all day. Good thing she'd had them add a dessert to her to-go order when she got there. As far as ever accepting a dinner date—or *any* date—with her favorite tech, she just wasn't sure. What if something went wrong and messed up the professional relationship they had? Finding a tech who could do what he could just sounded like more work than it was worth.

She parked her Harley and pulled her dinner order from the saddlebag. She entered the kitchen through the pantry, setting the bag of food and the folder from Anderson on the countertop. She was opening the bag when she glanced across the room and she stopped.

"*Damn it!* Lost two more." She walked over, staring at the dead fish in the aquarium. She shook her head, mumbling out loud, "Why do I even *fuckin'* bother?"

She grabbed the scooper and captured both of them in one shot, tapping the extra water off before heading toward the bathroom.

"I don't blame you guys—hanging together, safety in numbers and all." She lifted the lid to the toilet and dumped them in. "Didn't really help ya, though, did it?"

She closed the lid and flushed, then returned the scooper to the aquarium area, pondering whether or not she should try again. Maybe not. At this point, she felt like she was single-handedly killing off the telescope goldfish community. She'd always thought they were so cool, ever since she was a kid. Their huge eyes and egg-shaped bodies. She'd read up on them to make sure she would give them everything they needed: just enough food but not too much, a clean place to live, and nothing they would impale their eyes on. Despite the fact that their eyes were huge, they actually had rather poor eyesight. She'd never seen them swimming funny, like sideways or whatever, so they probably weren't sick. Maybe just a birth defect.

She grabbed a plate and some utensils from the cabinets and a beer from the refrigerator. She removed the food from the to-go container and added it to the plate. She grabbed everything and headed over to her sofa and TV. Her head was too busy with everything she'd learned earlier in the day, and sitting and watching something with action or violence always cleared up her thoughts, and sometimes even gave her new ideas.

CHAPTER 6

L IONEL WHITLOCK WAS A CRAFTY BASTARD. THAT WAS obvious, looking all the way back through his college transcripts.

Jacqui had been up since 4:00 a.m., unable to sleep anymore with all the unknowns floating around in her head. She'd always found that when sleeping was an issue, the best remedy was a hard workout and a new project. So here she was, at almost six in the morning and already deep into learning what made Lionel tick. Find out what *made* him to learn how to *break* him.

Lionel Whitlock attended the University of Georgia, majoring in international relations and affairs, and marketing and marketing management. Okay, so he was smart. Probably why her father started a company with him. But where had it all gone wrong? Anderson had mentioned something about Lionel wanting to get involved with a particular international company and her father hadn't, something about their business reputation being shady.

She pulled up the company's history online and discovered a few issues with previous employees, grievances, and other things. People had been fired, and from everything Jacqui could find, including attempted lawsuits against the company, the people couldn't seem to get any traction or anyone to really take their side and believe them. Trumped-up charges without merit was the final call.

Maybe that was why Lionel had wanted to work with them, to merge with that company. They worked to get whatever they needed to support and protect their bottom line. That was ruthless; in fact, it was definitely on the same page as killing off your partner and your own flesh and blood should one or more decide they didn't want to support you. *Fuck, that's cold.*

She opened another browser and focused on images of her father and her uncle at different fundraising events and company celebrations. Lionel appeared to be several inches shorter than her father but still athletic looking. It looked like even in his midthirties, he was starting to get gray hair around his temples, sprinkled through his natural auburn color. Studying the image on the screen, she magnified it more, and there was definitely something amiss behind his steely-blue eyes.

They looked so happy and content working with each other in so many of the pictures. It didn't look like Lionel had ever married. Another browser: *ah, yes, here we go.* Divorced. She pulled up the court records and noticed that *irreconcilable differences* was the reason noted for the divorce, although Lionel had offered a huge alimony settlement. *Huh, wonder where that aunt is now?*

She pulled up a few more browsers but found no history on social media. She'd found a couple of pictures with the same woman standing next to Lionel at a few events, but nothing after the death of her parents. Maybe Lionel's wife had suspected him, so she filed for divorce, and then Lionel, wanting all his secrets to be kept, had her killed too. Brilliant, really, when you consider how it could better the situation. Divorce the wife but pay out a large sum for alimony, only to then have your wife killed for far less than what the total alimony would have been. She hated to give the devil his dues but *damn, brilliant*. Then she found it—the death certificate of the woman who'd been married to Lionel. She'd gone on vacation in the Bahamas and had drowned in a boating accident while waterskiing. *Coincidence?* Doubtful, especially after everything she'd learned.

It was clear the man who'd had her parents killed was diabolical and twisted. Fortunately, she had no problem playing in that arena. Nope. She would find out all she could and take this *bastard* down.

Jacqui's phone rang and she grabbed it, smiling when she saw the caller ID.

"Hello?"

"Jacqui, it's Denner."

"So I see. What's up?"

"I just wanted to let you know your new truck is going to be ready soon whenever you want to swing by." He paused. "Oh, and I might have a buyer for your old rig."

"Wow, that was fast."

"Yeah, this guy was looking for something not-so-pretty on the outside but with more power than usual under the hood."

"And he's agreed to my price?" She reached over and grabbed the sheets with the two bounty jobs that had come across her fax earlier that evening, scanning through them again.

"Actually, he was so happy about what was under the hood and a few of the other amenities, he offered an additional five hundred."

"*Damn.* Well, tell him I said thank you."

"I was thinking I could take you out to celebrate, maybe tomorrow night?"

She smiled. "Denner, how many times have I told you? Besides, I'm going to be out of town, working the next few days, remember?"

"Oh yeah. Okay, cool." He sounded deflated. "I'll finish the new rig up and close the deal for you."

"Thanks, and don't forget about your twenty percent."

"Oh, I won't." He paused. "Jacqui?"

"Yeah."

"Stay safe." He ended the call.

She looked at her phone and set it back down on the desk, staring at it for a moment. She smiled. Maybe one day she would be ready for love, or whatever presented itself to her that was appealing enough to hold her attention. Not that Denner didn't or couldn't hold her attention—there was something about him. But now just wasn't the time, especially with a mad ex-uncle on the loose. Nope. That definitely was first priority on the list of things to do.

CHAPTER 7

JACQUI CIRCLED THE ESTABLISHMENT A COUPLE OF TIMES before backing her truck into a space on the side of the lot, giving her a perfect view of the front and rear entrances of the building. She left the engine on while she got a feel for the foot traffic at that time. She'd been doing a little recon for the past two days ever since Stuart Greeley's name had popped up on her fax machine. He was a thirty-five-year-old low-level courier moving stolen goods but, according to her sources, no real threat, which would be a nice change.

After about ten minutes, she moved her truck forward and reparked it parallel to the side of the building, backing it in close to the rear door. She knew this exit was in the same hallway as the bathrooms, which would be perfect for detainment and a fast getaway. She also knew Greeley was still inside.

She slid out of her truck and locked the door. She released the latch on the rear gate but left it in the upright position. She walked around to the front of the building and entered, moving straight toward the bar and spotting her mark immediately. Greeley was enjoying a whiskey at the bar. He was just under six feet and looked to weigh in around one hundred and eighty pounds. He was deeply tanned and wore faded jeans and an untucked button-up shirt. He also looked like he really needed a bath.

Greeley looked over at her as she approached him, and she smiled.

"Well, hey there, pretty girl. Can I buy you a drink?" He grinned at her when she hopped up on a stool two seats from his.

"Sure, thank you. Whiskey, please." She nodded at the bartender. *When in Rome.*

"Ooh, I *like* that." Greeley grinned. "A *whiskey* girl."

The bartender set a glass down in front of her and added whiskey.

"I like all kinds of things." She picked up her glass. "Thanks."

"Oh, well, maybe when I get back from the li'l boys room, you can tell me what else you like." He leered at her, and she mustered a smile.

"Cool." She winked, allowing him to pat her arm before he walked away.

"You sure you got this, Bleu?" The bartender looked skeptical.

"Yep!" She tossed the whiskey back and set down the shot glass hard. She hopped off the barstool, leaving a twenty by the empty. "Thanks, Merle."

"Anytime. I'll keep the path clear for ya."

Jacqui moved to the rear of the building, heading down the hall where the bathrooms were located. She waited at the entrance of the hallway to block the exit. She pulled her retractable stick, holding it down tightly against her leg, knowing she would most likely have to use it. They never went quietly unless they were already dead.

Greeley came out of the men's room, and his eyes lit up when he saw her standing there.

"Hey, couldn't wait for ole Greeley to return, could ya?"

"Not really." She smirked, extending the stick. "I've got laundry to do tonight."

Anger flashed behind his eyes when he saw the weapon and realized why she was really there.

"Ah, *damn* it!"

Greeley rushed her and she stepped to the side, tripping him. He went down, and when he attempted to get back up, she swiftly delivered a blow with the stick across his upper back and shoulders with a left backhand. He crumpled down again, and she put a knee in his back and grabbed his arms, securing them with a zip tie.

"Come on. Up we go."

Jacqui tucked the weapon back into her pants pocket. He stood, grumbling under his breath the entire time. She headed out the back door with him, walking him to the rear of the truck.

"Oh, *hey*, lady. Are you really gonna stick me in the back?"

"Yes I am."

"But maybe I could sit up front with you and we could talk or *somethin'*." His eyes pleaded with her.

"I cannot express how much I *don't* want that to happen." She dropped the gate. "Come on, get in."

Greeley closed his eyes a moment and grumbled under his breath again while he rolled into the back of the truck. She secured the gate and walked toward the front. She glanced around and noticed a few pairs of curious eyes watching her, and she understood why. It wasn't every day you saw a woman ordering a large man to get into the back of a truck wearing zip ties.

Jacqui slid into the driver's seat and turned the engine over. She pulled away from the building and maneuvered the vehicle out of the parking lot toward the drop-off location. She was glad this was the only job she had today and even happier it had gone smoothly. She really did have laundry to do; plus, she needed to map out the fastest route for tomorrow morning's drive to New Orleans. She wished her new truck were going to be ready. That bed slider was really going to come in handy in the future. *Some of these bastards are heavy.*

CHAPTER 8

ALI HABIBI MOVED DOWN THE HALL TOWARD THE OFFICE of his new boss. Well, *fairly* new boss. Lionel Whitlock had hired him six months ago for special projects and in-depth web searches on various subjects. The pay was great and so were the hours. Whitlock was intense and extremely business minded. Ali couldn't recall if he'd ever seen the man smile, but overall, he seemed like a decent guy.

Ali stood just outside the open doorway while Whitlock finished a phone call.

"Come in, please." The man gestured for him to enter while he hung up the phone. "You're not in the middle of anything, I hope, because I've got a special project for you."

"No, sir, I'm free. How can I assist you?" Ali entered the office and stood on the opposite side of the desk.

"I'm looking for someone, but I don't have a lot for you to go on." Whitlock leaned forward, handing over a large manila envelope. "There's a name inside, and I need all the information you can find on them."

"Yes, sir. How soon would you like this information?"

"Forty-eight hours." Whitlock stared at him for a moment. "I also need this conversation and anything you find kept between us, understood?"

"Yes, sir." Ali nodded and walked out, smiling at Margie, who was sitting at her desk just outside Whitlock's office.

"Good afternoon, Margie." Ali nodded.

"How are ya, kiddo?" Her voice and accent were always a comfort to him.

"I'm good, thank you. Got a new project."

"I see that."

Her phone rang and she answered it.

Ali turned and moved down the hall to take the stairs like he normally did, back down to the third floor. He stopped off to grab some coffee on the way back to his office. He sat behind his desk and opened the envelope, removing a single sheet of paper. In fact, that was the only thing inside. *Not a whole lot to go on. Man, Whitlock wasn't kidding.* A single name on the sheet of paper: *Jacqueline Indigo DeMott.* He shrugged and opened up the notepad app on his laptop and got started on the new project.

CHAPTER 9

J ACQUI HAD MADE GOOD TIME, DESPITE CONSTRUCTION happening on the I-10, which was still the fastest route. She had always wanted to come to New Orleans when Mardi Gras was happening, at least just once. It was just all about timing. She located a parking spot after grabbing some food on a side street offering residential and business parking so she could blend right in. She double-checked the address and couldn't believe it when she found a spot right in front of the house, so loading him up wouldn't be an issue. She'd learned through her connection, and some incredibly stupid confessions on social media, that the mark had a standing appointment at this young woman's house every Thursday around 4:00 p.m., lookin' for that *afternoon delight*. She chuckled to herself, remembering the lyrics to the song. Way before her time, but she did have a thing for seventies and eighties music, and some sixties too.

Jacqui spotted him rounding the corner, an enthusiastic rhythm in his step as he jogged up the stairs to the front door.

She watched as the front door opened and he stepped inside. She caught a glimpse of the woman and knew she wouldn't be an issue.

Jacqui slipped off her leather jacket and turned it inside out before placing it on the floorboard to blend in. A black tank top and her dark-brown Carhartt pants were standard attire on these kinds of jobs. All the pockets in the pants were extremely handy, and the tank top just gave her more freedom to move. She quietly opened her door and slipped out of the truck, pushing the door closed enough so that it latched slightly. She walked to the rear of the vehicle and unlatched the tailgate, leaving it up.

The white fence in front of the house was unusually high, around six feet tall, and there were two gates to choose from to enter the yard to the house. She decided to go through the one farthest from the front door. She pushed it open, stepping through quickly before closing the gate again. She crept quietly along the side of the house, locating a small window to a daylight basement. She pulled out her SOG Kiku and popped the lock on the window, pushing it open. She squeezed through the opening and dropped to the floor, remaining in a crouched position to listen to the noises upstairs. She heard some chatter and laughter, but that was all for the moment. She really wanted to grab him before they got busy.

Jacqui moved up the stairs and listened at the door to get a location on them. They were just about to move up to the second floor, so she needed to speed it up. She pushed the door open and moved quickly through the kitchen, still tracking their voices.

The woman was standing on the bottom stair, facing the man, teasing him as he walked toward her, grinning from ear to ear.

"Morgan Decker, I need you to come with me." Jacqui winked.

"Oh *shit!*" Morgan turned and moved quickly toward the front door.

"Hey!" The young woman looked pissed.

Before Morgan could reach the doorknob, Jacqui pulled a chain whip off her left wrist and swung it once counterclockwise, wrapping the end around his ankle. She pulled hard, dropping him to the ground while he was swearing up a storm. She pulled the Taser from her right pants pocket and touched it to his back when he got up on his knees. Stunned for a moment, this gave Jacqui the opportunity to come in with a rear naked choke hold until he went limp. She released him and he fell forward.

"What the *fuck,* lady? That's my customer." She scurried over to Jacqui with her hands on her hips.

"Exactly, which is illegal in this *fine* state." Jacqui turned to face her. "So instead, how about you accept this charitable contribution from me and keep this just between us, *'kay?*"

Jacqui handed her six hundred dollars. "Oh, and you probably shouldn't count on him to visit in the future." She turned her attention back to the man on the floor, turning him over and adding some zip ties to his wrists.

"Geez, lady, thanks." The woman eyeballed the cash like it was Christmas. "What's your name?"

"I don't have one." She rolled her eyes at the woman's confusion. "I was never here. Got it?"

"Yeah, okay." She tucked the cash down the front of her bra. "Hey, how are you gonna get him out of here?"

"Using my legs."

Jacqui bent down and unwrapped the chain from his ankle, securing it back on her wrist. She straddled the man's body and leaned forward to pull him into an upright position. She squatted down after lifting his arms up and grabbed the middle of his body. Still crouched, she stepped back, allowing his upper body to fall forward, and she used her legs to stand up, hoisting his body over her right shoulder in a standard fireman's carry.

"Can you grab the door for me, please?" Jacqui asked.

The woman looked astounded as she moved quickly to open the door. She didn't know who this chick was, but after seeing her manhandle Morgan, she didn't wanna know. Maybe it was time to look into another line of work. *Perhaps beauty college.*

"Thanks."

Jacqui moved down the stairs and paused to listen to the foot traffic on the other side of the fence before opening the gate. It was clear, so she stepped out and moved swiftly to the rear of her truck. She dropped the tailgate with one hand and dropped Morgan on the bed, rolling him over on his side. He probably wouldn't stay in that position for long, but that was fine. She just needed to get the hell out of New Orleans as soon as possible. Besides, his comfort? Not really her top priority.

Jacqui drove up to the location, happy to be back in Georgia. She opened the glove box and removed her weapon, then wrapped her adjustable belly holster around her waist and tightened it; Rosie was ready to go. She grabbed her leather jacket and pulled it on, leaving it open. The man who'd hired her was a real sleazeball, always looking her up and down like he'd rather pay her in trade. *Not even on my worst day.*

She slid out of the truck, smiling when she heard the thumping again coming from the rear of the vehicle. Decker had put out a lot of energy for at least half the time it took them to get back to Georgia, probably figuring he was about to be royally screwed. She dropped the tailgate and immediately stepped back. Some of those assholes had no problem kicking a person in the face, and she actually *liked* her face the way it was.

"About time you let me out." Decker rolled to the edge and out onto the ground, hitting the dirt with a thud. "Where the *hell* are *we*?"

He stood up, and when he recognized the building, he started to bolt. Jacqui swept his legs, and he hit the ground again, grunting this time.

"You *fuckin'* bitch! You can't take me in there!" Decker pleaded on his knees. "That man is *crazy*."

"Well, I'm a bit unsettled myself, but what are you gonna do." She grabbed him under his right arm. "Up you go."

They walked together across the dirt parking lot and up the side stairs of the building, with Decker asking her to change her mind the entire time. She knew she couldn't; plus, she'd heard it all before. People just didn't get it. If they really screwed up, bad things were going to happen. Somehow, because she was a woman, they expected her to be more understanding and show more compassion, which just wasn't her style. She had a job to do and a professional reputation to uphold, even if some of the people who hired her for the jobs had no idea whether they were hiring a man or a woman. J Bleu. It worked well for her.

Inside, they walked down a long hallway, and she knocked on an office door at the end. Personally, she couldn't wait to wrap this job up. The building smelled like filth, despite the scent of fresh paint that got stronger the closer they got to Carter's office.

"Come in," a gravelly male voice said.

Jacqui opened the door to find Dexter Carter in all his putrid glory, sitting behind his desk, puffing on a cigar, with piles of cash spread out in front of him. It looked like he had lost more of his red hair, with only a few tufts on top and full coverage on the sides, making his forehead all the more prominent and more freckled. His blue eyes were clouded with redness and a hidden agenda. And of course, his attire was never impressive, what with his shirt always being at least a size and a half too small. She was really just hoping he'd stay seated today. The man always had his fly down. *As if* . . .

She immediately noticed one of the guys Mr. Carter referred to as *muscle* stepping out from behind the door and, after she noticed his arms, it seemed appropriate. He had the standard Mr. Clean look to him, except with a full beard and beady sinister eyes. The man was well over six feet and at least a couple of bills and change. His eyes roamed over Jacqui's body, and she felt a sudden desire to shoot him.

She also noticed a parrot in the corner in a rather small cage. *That's new.*

"Looks like your bird could use more room in his cage." She tightened her grip on Decker's arm.

"Well, Bleu, it's nice of you to finally join us this evening. Thought maybe Morgan got away from you." Carter sat back and puffed on his cigar.

"*Really?* 'Cause considering I just made a twelve-hour-plus round trip and it's not even close to midnight, I'd say I'm doing pretty *damn* well." She smiled. "And I know you're a bit of a night owl, so cut the crap. Here's your bounty." She pushed Decker to the side and took several steps forward.

"Well, it's unfortunate, but I don't need or want him any-more." He flicked a few ashes in her general direction. "You should've just dropped his ass in the Mississippi on the way out of town."

"*Arw, drop his ass,*" the parrot mimicked.

She heard a heavy thud and a grunt behind her, and turned to see the muscle had put Decker on the ground and he was grimacing in pain.

"*What?* That's bad business, changing the parameters in the middle of the deal, Carter. It's bad for your reputation." Her anger flared.

"You think I give a *shit* about my reputation? We ain't workin' at the Plaza, princess." He took another puff on his cigar.

"This was more face time than I usually provide for this type of job. You need to compensate me for altering the agreement."

"Listen here, little girl . . ." Carter leaned across his desk. "Don't you ever come in here makin' demands of me, do you understand? You'll be lucky if I ever hire you again." His squinty eyes slithered up and down her body. He slid a stack of cash to the front edge. "Now, take your money and get your *hot li'l ass* out of my office before I have Tucker there teach you how to *behave.*"

"Arw, hot ass," the parrot mimicked again.

Her jaw tightened as she glanced at her payment and the rest of the money spread out on the desk.

Fuck this!

She shook her head and turned to leave, hearing laughter behind her. She paused, turning to look back at the sad, pudgy man, a twisted smirk on his round face.

"Trade, it is." Carter chuckled. "Tucker?"

Jacqui spun around, pulling her retractable stick from a leg pocket on the left side of her pants and hitting the button to extend it. She struck Tucker as he approached with everything she had, breaking the radius bone in his right arm. Tucker held his arm, growling in pain while Jacqui's second swing to his left side took out a few ribs to immobilize him. He dropped to the floor. She pulled Rosie and spun around, firing a shot at the sleazebag behind the desk and hitting him in his right shoulder.

"Damn it, you *fuckin' bitch!"* Carter held his arm close to his body, wincing in pain.

"Arw, fuckin' bitch!" the bird squawked from the corner.

Jacqui continued pointing her gun at Carter, slowly walking toward the desk. "I don't like gettin' screwed, so here's what you're gonna do." She looked at the pile of money in front of him. "You're gonna slide an additional two thousand dollars of that money to the front edge of the desk, and then you're going to sit there and bleed while I leave, got it?" She retracted the stick and put it away.

Carter nodded, letting go of his arm long enough to follow her instructions.

She gathered up the money and tucked it inside her jacket, then zipped it back up.

"I do agree with you on one thing," she stated.

"Oh yeah, what's that?"

"Don't ever hire me again. If I have to come back here, I'll kill you."

"What the hell am I gonna do with him?" He pointed at the bounty on the floor.

She turned to leave and popped a couple of rounds into Decker's back before walking out.

"Problem solved."

Jacqui moved quickly down the hall and out of the building. She jumped in her truck and hauled ass out of the parking lot. *Fuck!* That was *not* how she liked doing business. Too many witnesses left who knew her face and skill set. She didn't need to take any more jobs from that piece of shit. Hopefully, tonight's events wouldn't come back to bite her in the ass.

CHAPTER 10

THAT BUZZING NOISE NEEDED TO STOP.

Damn it!

Jacqui finally realized it was her phone.

"What?" she answered, frustrated that it had woke her up.

"Bleu?"

"Who the hell is this? What time is it?" She rolled over, trying to focus on the clock.

"It's Denner. Everything all right?"

"Um, sure. Just a late night." Her throat was dry and her voice raspy.

It was almost ten o'clock in the morning, and she was still in bed. She never slept that late.

"I need a shower and some coffee." She sat up, immediately pressing her hand to her aching head, realizing she was still on the phone. "Oh, *shit*. Sorry, what's up?"

"I just wanted to let you know I'm almost done with the truck, if you wanted to swing by and take a look at it. That is, if you're feeling up to it."

"Oh, sure. I just need—"

"A shower and some coffee—and some food, if I'm reading you correctly." His smile came through the phone as he finished her sentence.

"Oh, *damn,* please don't mention food right now. Oh, gotta go!"

She ended the call and rushed to the bathroom, happy it was just a false alarm.

Jacqui got in the shower, allowing the warmth to soothe her aching head. She knew better than to drink that much whisky, but last night's debacle had really done a number on her. She'd been doing this kind of work now for two years, and for only being twenty-three years old, she had managed to gain a good following for getting work and a solid reputation for always being professional. Now that might have all been wiped out with one job.

Fuck. She should've just killed Carter. Who the hell would've known either way?

She finished her shower and dried off before throwing on her standard apparel. Some women loved their purses—not Jacqui. All she needed were her Carhartts with all the pockets, her brown leather jacket, and brown motorcycle boots. She put her wet hair in a braid, knowing it would be mostly dry by that night.

Now all she needed was coffee and a greasy burger, and she knew exactly where to get it. She also grabbed her water bottle and refilled it before heading out to her truck.

The burger was satisfying, but she just couldn't seem to get enough coffee, so she grabbed another one to go on her way to see the new truck. Once there, she walked into the building and found Denner sitting at the small desk in the corner.

"Well, she lives." He chuckled and stood, walking over to the counter. "How are you feeling?"

"Better, thanks." She set her cup and sunglasses on the counter and looked at him.

"Everything all right?"

"Yeah, why do you ask?" She picked up her coffee and took a long sip.

"Because in all the time I've known you, I've never known you to have a hangover." He studied her a moment. "You know you can talk to me."

"I'm fine." He didn't look convinced, so she went on. "It's just . . . I had a job yesterday, and the one who hired me made changes after the fact."

"Did you explain to him that would normally be considered bad business?"

"Yes I did—in my own special way."

She smirked, and he couldn't help but laugh. He knew something had gone down, but he also knew she would probably never share.

"Well, I'm glad you're okay. I do have some unfortunate news regarding the new truck."

"*Damn*, now what?" She stared at him. "Sorry."

He chuckled. "It's fine—it's just one of the components needed to secure a part was missing from the kit, so I sent Brady out to grab a new one and he'll install it right away."

"Oh, okay. Thanks." She smiled.

"In the meantime, why don't we go grab an early dinner?"

"I don't think so." She grabbed her glasses, slipped them back on, and picked up her coffee before turning to walk out the door. "Hey, can you maybe just drive the new truck out to me when it's done and then you can drive the old one back?" She glanced back at him.

"Sure, I can do that."

"Thanks." She reached for the door.

"Why can't I take you to dinner?"

She turned and smirked. "I like eating alone."

"Liar." He chuckled and raised an eyebrow. "I've seen you looking me over."

She walked back over to the counter, sliding her glasses halfway down her nose. "I study people. I study all people, everybody." She placed her coffee cup and hands on the counter, taking a stance.

"And now you're just rambling." He grinned. "Come on, Jacqui."

She shook her head. "Gotta go." She picked up her coffee and moved toward the door.

"Bleu?"

She turned and looked at him, clearly more annoyed. *"What?"*

"You're not the only one who studies people." He winked and laughed when she rolled her eyes and pushed her shades into place before walking out.

Denner stepped out from behind the counter, stopping in front of the door. He watched as she made her way to her truck parked across the lot, ignoring the shuffle of George's boots when he came in from the shop.

"Still can't get a date?" George asked, peering over his shoulder out the side window.

"Shut up."

"Don't give up, man. I really do believe you're wearing her down."

George tapped him on the back of his left shoulder with his fist before walking back out toward the shop.

"Oh, Brady just called and said he finally found that part. He should be back here in an hour."

"Thanks, George."

Denner never turned around. He just kept watching Jacqui until she drove away. For someone so young, he could tell she'd been through way too much.

CHAPTER 11

J ACQUI RAN A FEW MORE ERRANDS, PICKING UP ITEMS SHE was getting low on at home. Since it was such a trek, being well stocked was never a bad idea. It was nice of Denner to agree to dropping her new truck off to her later that night. She felt like the symptoms of her hangover were almost gone, and now all she needed was a good meal to complete the process. Well, a good meal and a little hair of the dog. Funny how that seemed to help.

Leaving the last store carrying three bags of groceries, she was happy none of them had to be refrigerated, since she wasn't heading straight home. She was hungry and needed to eat soon, if only to improve her mood. She had rounded the corner and was heading toward her truck when she heard the faint cries of kittens coming from the alley. She stopped, noticing a middle-aged man wearing grimy clothes, standing in front of a dumpster. He picked up a box from the ground and set it on top. Rage filled Jacqui when she realized the tiny cries were coming from inside the box. *Oh, hell no.*

"Excuse me, sir? What are you doing with those kittens?"

"None of your damn business, lady," he called over his shoulder. "Now *fuck off.*"

Jacqui moved farther into the alley and set her bags down. "Hey, there's no way in hell I'm gonna let you throw those kittens away. You should take them to a shelter or give them away outside a grocery store." She stopped about five feet away from him.

"What the hell do you care? Just piss off and mind your own damn business." He slid the box over slightly, tossing the lid up on the opposite side. He turned to look at her. "Besides, they're just *animals.*"

"Yep, and so are you." *And there goes the last bit of my tolerance.*

Jacqui pulled Rosie out and shot the man in his right knee, dropping him to the ground. He lay there, moaning in pain, mumbling under his breath. She quickly put the gun away and walked over to collect the box on top of the dumpster. She pulled it down and looked inside to see four kittens, no more than four weeks old.

"What happened to their mother?" she asked.

"Damn little *bitch* ran out in the road and got tagged by a car. Stuck me with these little *shits.*" He groaned again. "You *fuckin'* shot me. What the hell is wrong with you?"

"You should be nicer to animals."

She walked away with the box, pausing to pick up her bags.

"Wait, you just gonna leave me here?" the man called after her.

"Call it karma, *bitch.*"

Jacqui walked out of the alley, moving quickly to her truck. She set the box of kittens on the passenger side of the seat and her bags in the back. She climbed in behind the wheel and turned the engine over, deciding to put some distance between her and the alley as fast as possible. She drove for about half a mile and then pulled over to locate the nearest animal shelter. The thought of keeping some of the kittens crossed her mind, but who was she kidding? *I can't even keep goldfish alive.*

She located a no-kill shelter that was just down the road from her favorite steak house. She dropped the kittens off at the shelter, telling the employees she'd found them in an alley, which was true. She left out the part about the jerk attempting to throw them away. The shelter happily accepted the kittens, and she left feeling better. *Is it wrong that saving kittens and shooting an asshole lifted my spirits? Hard to say.*

She pulled into the parking lot of the steak house, parking her truck on the edge of the lot. She backed it in like she always did before turning off the engine. She sat and watched the foot traffic moving in and out of the restaurant, seeing if there was anything noteworthy. Everything seemed rather calm tonight, which she was thankful for. She pulled Rosie and the belt holster off, unloading the weapon before tucking it in the glove box. She felt like she'd already had a full day.

She got out of her truck and walked across the parking lot. It sounded crazy, but she knew a least at little whisky would help balance her out. Plus, it was always good with a rare steak. She entered the restaurant, happy to see her favorite seat available at the end of the bar. It was perfect because it seemed to offer more space away from the other customers and a great view of what was happening in the entire room. She was also happy to see Marty was working. He was a nice guy and always ready to lend a hand if anybody bothered her.

You could tell from his build and the way he carried himself he'd probably played ball in his youth. He looked to be in his midforties, with a neatly trimmed salt-and-pepper beard and a clean-shaven head. His friendly smile and warm brown eyes always made her feel welcome.

"Hey, Jacqui, how you doin' tonight?"

"I'm okay, Marty, how are you?" She stepped up and sat on a barstool.

"I'm good. Your usual?"

"No, I'm going with Johnnie Gold tonight, a straight double." She smiled when he raised his eyebrow. "Rough night."

Marty chuckled. "You got it." He grabbed the bottle and a glass and poured. "Anything to eat?"

"How about the six-ounce Renegade Sirloin with Redrock Grilled Shrimp, and a side of broccoli?"

"Broccoli? Wow, you *did* have a rough night. Rare on the steak?"

"Yes, thank you."

"Comin' up." He set her drink down in front of her and headed off to turn her order in.

She picked up her glass and closed her eyes, holding it under her nose to savor the sweet honey and creamy vanilla flavors. *Mmm, heaven.* She took a sip and smiled, glancing across the bar to the TV mounted on the wall. The Braves were playing and seemed to be doing well so far this season.

"Well, *hel-lo.*" A gravelly voice disrupted her peace. "Hey there, *pretty* thing. Can I buy you a drink?"

"No thanks, I'm good." She glanced in the direction of the voice and realized it was coming from the same man who'd cut her off with his truck the other night in the parking lot.

He was over six feet tall, with a dark beard graying around his chin and thick, dark bushy eyebrows peeking out from under a camouflaged ballcap. He was sporting a few gold chains while wearing a wifebeater under his grimy-looking dark overalls. *No chance of seeing him on the Paris runway.*

"Mm-hmm," he grunted, leaning back to check out her ass. "My God, I don't think I've ever seen Carhartts look so sweet as they do huggin' that fine *ass. Damn*, baby, you're *packin!*"

"Wow, so poetic," she stated dryly, wishing she'd ordered to go. She just wasn't up to dealing with another asshole tonight.

"I just can't seem to keep my eyes off ya." He continued leering at her.

"Well, there are a few ways to remedy that. You could either leave, avert your eyes, or"—she picked up her steak knife and twirled it, looking back at him—"I could remove them for you."

"*Man*, there's no need to be such a *bitch*." He settled onto the stool next to her. "I'm just tryin' to show you a good time."

"Funny, I was having a better time before you showed up." She spotted Marty heading over and signaled with her eyes that there was an issue. He missed nothing.

"Hey, Mack, what'll it be tonight?"

"Hey, Mart, give me a brew and a shot on the side, and see if you can get this *li'l* girl to give me her number." His eyes traveled back over to Jacqui.

"All right, Mack, take it easy." Marty set a beer and a shot down in front of him. "Let's leave the other customers alone, *'kay?*"

The man grunted, throwing the shot back and then sucking down his beer faster than should have been humanly possible.

"I'll grab your food," Marty said to Jacqui.

"Thanks." She looked back at the TV but didn't really feel like she should take her eyes completely off the moron to her left.

"You know . . ." He leaned over, the smell of liquor floating across the air. "You look *familiar* to me, like I've *had* you before." He raised his eyebrows. "Or maybe *you* were just in my last *wet* dream."

"Nope, not me." She looked him dead in the face, maintaining eye contact. This piece of *shit* was starting to irritate her.

"Here you go." Marty set her food down in front of her. "Hope you're hungry."

"So hungry I could kill." She winked at Marty, and he chuckled.

"Hey, Mack, how about I get you another round and we let the lady eat in peace." Marty was already pouring another beer and shot for the man.

"Peace?" Mack sneered and turned his body toward Jacqui, grabbing his crotch. "I've got a *piece* for ya *right* here."

Jacqui was just about ready to cut into her steak, knife in hand, when she smirked at the dirtbag. "Now, why would I settle for a small *hors d'oeuvre* when I got an *incredible* full meal in front of me?"

"That's it, *bitch!*" The man stood, towering over her.

"All right, Mack, get your drinks and move to the other side of the bar or leave." Marty leaned over the bar with his arm in front of the man, staring into his eyes. "Those are your choices."

"*Fine.*" He picked up his beer and Marty grabbed his shot. "You *aren't* all that, *anyway.*"

Jacqui watched as he moved around to the other side, where Marty told him to sit. Sadly, now he was glaring at her from straight across the bar. Fortunately, his new location made him easier to track. She dug into her steak, savoring the flavor and juices, doing her best to ignore the man. Thankfully, he now seemed to be paying more attention to the Braves than anything else.

Jacqui was just finishing her broccoli when Marty gave her a nod and wandered back over.

"I'm so sorry about that mess earlier." He reached for her empty plate.

"It's cool—and, hey, thanks for not using my name." She winked.

"You got it. That guy is always giving some woman a difficult time. Hey, how about some dessert, on the house?" He grinned when she laughed.

"Sure, thanks."

"I've got just the thing. Be right back."

She finished her drink while watching him disappear into the kitchen. The jerk across the way was still mostly focused on the game, which was a relief, but every now and then she could feel his eyes on her. She was grateful for Marty. He was like an uncle or big brother, depending on your age, always looking out for the women who came into the bar by themselves. She figured he probably had a sister or two, or perhaps daughters.

"Here you go, the Chocolate Stampede." He set a chocolate cake down with thick chocolate frosting, flanked by two small scoops of vanilla bean ice cream. There was chocolate drizzled over it and whipped cream on top.

"Holy crap. That looks delicious." She giggled like a little girl.

"Oh, it is. What would you like to drink with it?"

"Um . . ." She thought a moment. "Ooh, how about a shot of Chivas?"

"Oh, girl, I like your style." Marty grinned. "Coming up."

Jacqui dug into her dessert, forgetting all about her troubles for about twenty minutes. She paid her bill and decided she needed to leave, especially since the jerk across the way had taken a renewed interest in her.

"Thanks for everything, Marty." She slid off the stool. "See you next time."

"You got it. Take care."

She headed back toward the bathroom, noticing that the jerk was no longer at the bar. Good. Maybe he'd just called it a night. She rounded the corner and was heading into the women's bathroom when she felt a hand grab her ass, pushing her forward as the door swung open. She kept her footing, catching herself before her face hit the wall. She spun around, not at all surprised to see Mack blocking the door with his six-foot frame.

"O-*kay*, sweetie, now that were alone, *Big Mack* is going to teach you some manners."

"'Big Mack'?" She sneered, gauging the space she had to work with. "What *are* you, a *sandwich*?"

"Oh, *man*." He started undoing his belt and the fly on his

pants. "I've got something for that smart-ass mouth of yours, and then I'm gonna *fuck* you till you show some respect."

"If that *thing* comes anywhere near my mouth, I guarantee you won't be leaving with it." She smirked.

"You *fuckin' cun—*"

Mack lunged forward and was met with her left foot kicking him in the crotch and a right hook to his jaw. He dropped to the floor, groaning, and she walked around him to leave the bathroom.

Jacqui walked back around the corner and flagged Marty down.

"Hey, I thought you left."

"Yeah, well, that was the plan, but I have a long drive, so I thought I would use the bathroom first. Mack thought I needed assistance, though."

"Oh no." Marty moved quickly around the bar. "Are you all right?"

"Except for the fact I still need to go to the bathroom, sure." She gestured around the corner. "Can you clear a path for me please?"

"Yeah, I'll take care of it."

"Thanks."

Like most men in the area, Marty was tough as nails and not someone you wanted to mess with. She was glad he was on her side.

He came back around the corner, shaking his head. "He's gone. I checked all the stalls."

"Wow, okay, thanks." She moved past him, heading to the restroom.

"You seem surprised."

"Well . . ." She turned and grinned. "I nailed him pretty good. Guess I need to work on my kicks." She glanced below his belt and chuckled when he winced. "Thanks again."

"Anytime."

Jacqui used the bathroom and then headed out to the parking lot. She walked quickly around a fenced wall and was heading straight for her truck when, all of a sudden, she was pushed forward toward the ground. She rolled out and was up on her feet when she saw the blade of a knife coming at her right side. It sliced through the front of her leather jacket in an upward motion, grazing her ribs under her right breast.

"*Ah!*" she moaned in pain, holding her side.

"That's right, *bitch*! *No* more playtime."

Jacqui exhaled, refocusing her attention back to the very large knife that had already gotten a piece of her. She had no idea how badly she was cut, only that it hurt like hell and she was pissed, cursing the fact she'd left her gun in the truck.

She needed to get away as soon as possible, preferably without any further damage. She pulled out her retractable stick from the pocket on the left side of her pants, extending it to block the next thrust of the knife and countering with a strike to his face with a right cross. The pain she felt on her right side only fueled her rage. She grabbed his shirt and head-butted him across the bridge of the nose, causing him to drop to his knees. She stepped back and swung her stick again, this time striking and breaking the knuckles on his right hand. He dropped his knife, and as his body pitched forward, he tried to lessen the impact by using both hands to catch himself. That's when she stepped forward, placing her boot on his broken hand and shifting her weight forward.

"Please, *please* don't kill me," Mack begged through grunts of pain.

She leaned forward. "The next *fuckin'* time a woman tells you she's not interested, you better listen, you *stupid motherfucker*."

"Yes. Yes I will, I promise. I'm sorry. *I'm so sorry*."

Jacqui stepped off his hand, slowly backing away. Once she'd put enough space between them, she turned and moved as fast as she could to her truck. She didn't think Mack would get up anytime soon, but she really didn't want to take the chance. She turned the engine over and drove out of the parking lot. She kept her right arm tucked into her body, applying what pressure she could on her ribs. *This is bad.*

CHAPTER 12

J ACQUI MANAGED TO DRIVE ALL THE WAY HOME WITHOUT passing out from the pain or blood loss; she was thankful for the hearty meal. She was also grateful everything she'd picked up while running errands could sit in the truck overnight, knowing there was no way she could carry anything. She was confused when she noticed a truck sitting alongside her gate; then she remembered Denner was stopping by to swap trucks with her. She entered the code on her watch to open the gate and pulled onto her property. She drove slowly down the driveway, glancing in her sideview mirror to see if he was following her. *This should be fun.*

She carefully stopped the truck and turned off the engine, remaining inside. She watched as he approached, and he didn't look happy. He opened the driver's-side door for her.

"*Damn it, Bleu.* I've been waiting here for ten minutes." He paused. "Didn't you remember I was bringin' the truck by?"

She managed a smile and tried to move, wincing in pain. "*Ah, sorry.* I was a little detained . . ."

"What happened? Are you okay?"

"Oh, sure. I'll be fine. If you could just help me inside."

She reached for him when he stepped forward, grabbing on to his body and holding on for dear life. When she took the first few steps, her knees buckled from the pain. He wrapped his right arm around her waist, accidentally grazing her injury.

"*Ah, damn,*" she hissed through her teeth.

"What the hell happened?"

"Less talking, more walking." Her hand gripped his side after she slid her arm around his midsection.

"Okay, I've gotcha."

He pushed the truck door closed and carefully walked with her to the house. She gestured where she needed to be and then activated the hand and retina scans.

Denner glanced around, noticing a solar generator near the house.

The door opened, and he helped her inside.

"Please, can you just help me upstairs and then you can go?"

"Yes I can, but I'm not leaving. You're hurt, so I'm gonna help you." They stopped walking after the door was closed, and he carefully picked her up in his arms. "You *know* I have medical field training, so I can help. Nothing I haven't seen before."

"Okay," she conceded as her head fell against his shoulder.

He paused when he reached the top of the stairs, momentarily wondering where to put her. She pointed and he moved across the room, carefully setting her down at the end of the bed.

"Medical supplies are in the bathroom," she whispered, wincing when she attempted to remove her jacket.

"Great."

He moved quickly toward the bathroom, flipping the overhead light on as he entered. He removed the liner from her small plastic garbage can, setting it aside before filling it with supplies he found in the medicine and linen cabinets. He came back into her room just as she was unzipping her jacket.

"Hey, wait. I'll help you." He grabbed her office chair to sit in, and after rolling it over to the bed, set the can with all the supplies near his feet on the floor.

"I can't believe that *asshole* destroyed my jacket." Attempting to pull her right arm out of the sleeve, she winced again and swore.

"Jacqui, please stop moving. I've got you." He looked into her eyes, melting a little when he saw they were a bit moist around the edges. "Tell me what happened." His voice was soothing and tender while he carefully removed her jacket.

"I was having dinner and getting harassed."

"Where were you?" He set the jacket off to the side.

"My favorite steak house on Dawson Road." She shifted, trying to give him better access to the injury. "The guy wouldn't take no for an answer. Marty even had to move him to the other side of the bar." She sucked in a breath as he tried rolling her tank top up to see the wound. "How bad is it?"

"Still not clear on that." He reached for the scissors. "I need to cut your tank top off. It's stuck in some blood."

"That's fine, just do it."

Jacqui rested her hands behind her on the bed, leaning back and holding on to the comforter while he cut through the front of her shirt. He slowly peeled the stuck fabric away from her skin and the gash.

"Seems like most of the bleeding has stopped, which is a good sign. It doesn't look as bad as it could've been." He reached for peroxide and gauze, then gently wiped the blood off to clear the hold on the fabric. "Looks like your jacket probably saved you. How big was this knife?"

She hissed a little when the peroxide made contact with the open wound. "Big enough to make me a little jealous it wasn't mine." She chuckled from the surprised look on his face. "I've got a thing for nice blades."

"Well now, I know what to get you for your birthday." He got back to work cleaning the area and studying the wound. "It looks like the blade actually skipped across the surface of your jacket, which is why the cut was not deeper." He stopped, his eyes getting a little wider, and he pulled back to look at her face.

"*What?*"

"Well, it's just . . . It appears you got cut underneath your bra line." He stopped.

"*And?*"

He cocked his head to the left, hesitating a moment. His eyes held a hunger that needed no explanation.

"*Oh*, for God's sake." She rolled her eyes, pulling her black fixed blade out from the sheath on the right side of her pants. She stuck it down the front of her sports bra and turned it ninety degrees, cutting through the fabric. She slipped the knife back into the sheath as the material fell away from her body, exposing her full, bare breasts right in his face.

Denner's eyes were huge. "Well, *that* wasn't in the field manual."

He shook his head a little to regain his focus before cleaning the wound and applying liquid skin and a bandage.

He knew his desire was obvious and something he could no longer hide as he gathered up all the bloody gauze, desperately trying not to stare at her naked breasts. He did notice the pulse on the side of her neck was beating faster than normal, matching the rhythm of his own.

"I should go get cleaned up," she stated, looking into his eyes.

"Yes, of course." He rolled the chair back so she could stand.

Jacqui stood slowly and turned away from him. He watched as she walked into the bathroom and closed the door.

Denner leaned back in the chair, his hands holding the sides of his head while he attempted to regain his composure. *Haven't taken her to dinner and yet . . .*

He chuckled to himself, standing to move around the room a little, attempting to shake off his excitement. He directed his attention to his surroundings, admiring the simplistic feel of the bedroom furniture, particularly her headboard, with its built-in shelves. There were a few books and trinkets, which surprised him. She didn't really seem like a "trinkets" kind of girl. There were two matching bedside tables with drawers and lamps on top, and a large matching dresser on the same wall as double barn sliding doors. The doors looked like they might open to look down into the center of the building. He turned, scanning the rest of the room, taking in the L-shaped desk area where he'd pulled the chair from. There were a couple of laptops and a printer/fax machine. There was also a large hutch to the left of the desk area about four feet wide. He laughed to himself, wondering what could possibly be inside.

Denner heard the sliding door to the bathroom open behind him, and when he turned, he saw Jacqui standing in the doorway wearing nothing but a pair of black panties and a cropped pink T-shirt with a kitten on the front that said *Me-wow*. Her bandage stretched across her ribs on the right, and loose whisps of her dark-auburn hair that had escaped her braid framed her beautiful face.

She smiled. "You've got blood on your shirt and your jeans." She walked toward him. "I can wash them for you."

He reached down, pulling on the hem of his shirt to get a better look, surprised he was able to take his eyes off her. "I could just throw everything out." He chuckled, looking back up into her face, her hungry eyes staring back at him. "Or we could decide later."

He reached up and pulled his shirt forward over the back of his head, dropping it to the floor. His heart jumped when he saw a coy smile come over her face as he unbuttoned his jeans. He slid the jeans down his legs, pulling his boots off at the same time. She stepped forward, placing her hands on his firm muscular chest, the warmth of his skin making her head spin. He reached down and grabbed her legs, lifting her up onto his hips. They stared into each other's eyes as he carried her over and sat on the edge of the bed, carefully supporting her back to hold her still. He slowly reached up, brushing a strand of hair away from her face. She studied his beard, tracing it with her fingertips, and she gasped a little, watching his lips part.

"So," he whispered, staring at her mouth, "when *can* I take you to dinner?"

"I've already eaten," she replied softly.

"Dessert?"

"Had that too." She smiled. "But . . ."

She leaned forward, kissing him slowly at first, moaning as his tongue caressed hers and his strong hands held her in place. She ran her hands through his hair on the side of his head, leaning deeper into the most incredible kiss she'd ever experienced. Her entire body was tingling, and she suddenly felt faint. She felt his fingertips sink deeper into her back as the kiss stopped.

"Jacqui?" he whispered. "Are you all right?"

"Lightheaded."

Everything was fading, and she was gone, falling forward into him.

He leaned back slightly, holding the outside of her legs and pressing them against his hips while he slowly stood. He walked around the side of her bed and carefully laid her down, admiring for a moment the mostly naked woman in front of him. *Damn!*

He reached diagonally across the foot of the bed and pulled the multicolored comforter up to cover her. She stirred a moment, and he couldn't help himself, bending down to kiss her forehead.

He turned and quietly walked downstairs to see what she had in the refrigerator. Juice would be best, but he also wanted to see what she had in the way of protein. He saw the large fish tank as he neared the kitchen but he couldn't see any fish inside. *Okay, there is definitely a story there.*

He glanced around the rest of the downstairs area, noticing a nice-size TV, coffee table, a sofa, and a club chair. Everything looked very clean and tidy. He opened the refrigerator and saw a fair amount of eggs, cheeses, and butter inside. He found the juice and located a protein bar inside the snack bin under one of the glass shelves. He chuckled while pouring the juice into a glass. He'd learned more about Jacqui in the past hour than in all the years he'd known her.

He walked back upstairs, setting the juice and protein bar on her nightstand. He couldn't help smiling as she stirred again. This woman was an enigma, and he liked it. She wasn't like any other woman he'd ever met before, which was just one of the reasons he was so captivated by her. She was beautiful and strong, and watching what she did just to enter her own house intrigued him even more.

He took a seat on the opposite side of the bed, studying her when her eyes flew open. "Easy there. You're okay." His voice was soothing.

"How long was I out?" she asked, looking at the clock, noticing the comforter covering her body.

"About ten minutes." He nodded at the juice and protein bar on her nightstand. "I hope you don't mind, but I kinda raided your kitchen, figuring you needed something to help with the blood loss."

She carefully sat up in bed, surprised she wasn't in more pain. She picked up the glass and drank, setting the protein bar in her lap. "Thanks, this will help." Her eyes fell on his muscular naked chest, painted with tattoos she hadn't really noticed before. She studied the sleeves on his arms and smiled at a few of the images.

"Some of these I got before I became a Ranger, and others came later." He grinned when he suddenly saw a hint of innocence behind her eyes, and then it was gone. "I take it you don't have any tattoos?"

She shrugged, setting the glass back on the nightstand. "Did you *see* any?" She bit into the protein bar, looking away for a moment.

"Honestly, I was doing my *damnedest* not to ogle you." He dropped his eyes, his grin broadening.

"And how did that work out for you?" she teased, feeling like she'd just gained the upper hand. She set the protein bar aside on the nightstand.

"I'm hangin' in there." He looked down and was reminded he was wearing only underwear. He laughed and looked back at her.

"Well . . ." She pushed the comforter off her legs and slowly slipped out of bed on the opposite side. She walked across the room to her desk. "If you don't have anywhere else to be tonight . . ." She hit the space bar and then entered a code on her laptop.

"No, I don't *have* anywhere else I need to be." He watched her carefully, sliding over to sit more in the center of the bed. He sat back and extended his legs out in front of him. "Question is, what do *you* want?" He smiled, winking when she looked over at him.

She hit a few more buttons after glancing at half a dozen cameras and turned to face him.

This man was special, and she knew it from everything he'd shown her in the past hour. Maybe it was time to let her guard down. She felt warmth spread through her as she watched his eyes slowly follow the curves of her body and then look back up at her face. She walked over to him, impressed by the fact that he was comfortable enough to sit back against her pillows on her bed, wearing nothing but his underwear. He reached out and caressed her left hip with his right hand, guiding her toward him. She placed her left knee on the bed beside him and gingerly extended her right leg over to straddle him, feeling the liquid adhesive that closed her wound pulling against her movements.

"I want *you*." She caressed the side of his face, settling down on his lap.

"Thank *God*."

He pulled her in for a kiss, holding her close with his left hand on her lower back as he gently pulled his knees up to support her. With his right hand, he reached behind her, caressing the smooth skin on her firm ass. His hands roamed over the sides of her body as he pushed her shirt up past her breasts, kissing them, something he'd wanted to do since they were bared to him. She pulled her shirt off over her head, reaching forward and pulling one of her knives from its sheath on the middle shelf.

She sat back and he froze when he saw the knife, putting his hands up.

She whispered, staring into his eyes, *"Relax."*

Jacqui reached behind her with her left hand and pulled the material of her thong away from her body while she methodically cut through the top of it with the knife. The material fell away and she sat up slightly, pulling it out from between them. She set the knife back on the shelf, leaning back to gaze into his eyes.

Denner pushed his underwear down his hips, and he

guided her back down to his lap. He entered her and the initial pressure made her shudder with pleasure.

"Oh *God*, it's been—"

"—so long," he groaned, finishing her sentence. *"Jacqui . . ."* He paused for a moment, caressing her face.

"Hmm." She leaned down and kissed him passionately, sinking into his warmth as she shifted her pelvis back and forth slowly.

"Careful, I don't want to hurt you."

"Oh, but it feels like it's so worth it right now." She held on to his shoulders, afraid to let go.

"Let me."

He placed his hands on her hips, allowing his fingertips to sink into her round ass. He gently applied pressure, maneuvering her hips to roll back and forth against his body. Her head fell back and she moaned loudly, grinding her pelvis against his. He cradled her body, supporting her more so she wouldn't strain herself. He watched her passion grow as her moans echoed across the ceiling of the room. Her fingertips dug into his shoulders as his hands caressed and supported her body, his own passion building up until he finally exploded. She cried out one last time before her body fell forward, her arms hugging his head to her chest, while she panted in his ear. Her moist skin burned even hotter where he dropped scorching kisses while trying to catch his own breath. They lingered in their embrace for several minutes, enjoying the heat they'd created together.

She slid off his lap and carefully stretched out on the bed beside him, wincing a bit in pain as she worked to find a comfortable position. She carefully rolled over on her left side to face him as he slid down on the bed.

He rolled over, facing her, matching her propped-up style. "So, tell me: Why the name Jacqui Bleu?"

"I've always loved the song." She glanced down. "The first time I heard it, with the reference to indigo eyes, I thought it was a sign."

He reached out and brushed a strand of hair out of her eyes, studying them a moment.

"And the spelling?"

"I like to be different; plus, it's a nod to the name my mother gave me." She sat up, planting her left hand on the bed to steady herself, looking across the room.

His patience was both unnerving and a blessing, allowing her to speak at her own pace. She glanced over at him and rolled her eyes, laughing when he did. Then her smile fell away and she slid back against the pillows carefully, bending her knees and pulling her legs into her chest. She sighed and shook her head.

"My life story thus far is horribly odd, to say the least." Her gaze remained down as she stared at her big toe.

He sensed trepidation and wondered if he was pushing too hard. "If you don't want to—"

"No, we should. I mean, I *should* tell you who I am." She dropped one of her knees down on the bed and smiled. "I think you've earned that."

He waited patiently.

"I never knew my parents. I was raised by Emma, my nanny, on the farm where she'd grown up. My mother gave me to her and told her to keep me safe and to raise me as her own." She paused a moment. "I was only three days old when my parents were murdered in cold blood. Emma got me out and kept me safe." She paused again, looking up at the ceiling as a few tears rolled down her cheeks. It didn't seemed to matter how old the story was; if you were sharing it with someone new who cared about you, the pain could return as if it had never left, like it was the first time you were feeling it.

He reached out, placing a soothing hand on her leg.

"When I was nine, I found the note my mother had written and the family photo album." She chuckled. "Apparently, my mother was big on tradition, so *yes*, she still had a physical book full of pictures. I felt hurt and confused. Emma was great, but suddenly I understood why I never felt like I was really part of their family."

"I'm so sorry. Why were they killed?"

Jacqui wiped the tears away, her eyes shifting back to cold and distant as she regained her composure. "Emma filled in the blanks with information she had overheard while working in the house. Apparently, my father and my mother's brother were in business together. My father didn't want some merger to happen, but my uncle kept pushing him to agree to it. When he didn't, my uncle had them killed, giving him the controlling shares in the company so he could move forward with the merger."

Denner sat up in the bed in disbelief. "Your *uncle* had his own sister killed because of some *fucking* business disagreement?"

She nodded.

"*Damn*, that's cold."

"Exactly." She smirked. "What my uncle doesn't know is, because I am the rightful heir to the DeMott holdings that were my father's, I could take over the company and force him out."

"Would that really be possible? I mean, is that what you want to do?"

"I don't know. I found a man who was my father's best friend and best man at their wedding, and he's a lawyer. He retired after my parents were killed." She smiled to herself. "He was there when they met. He was there when my parents fell in love." She stared off into the distance, unshed tears brimming her eyes.

"Hey, I'm here for whatever you need. You know, I used to be considered a *badass* back in my day." He winked at her.

"Oh, I know." She smirked, reaching up and brushing away her fresh tears. "Why do you think you're in my bed, mister?" She leaned over and kissed him.

"So, what exactly is this place?" He looked around and shook his head. "'Cause it's not like any other barn I've seen."

She smiled and her head fell back as she laughed.

"What?" He grinned, enjoying her laughter.

"I don't know. I haven't had that many people over, so I've never had to explain my home." She sighed. "Basically, I knew I needed to create something that offered durability and protection while being wrapped discreetly in a rather boring exterior."

He chuckled. "Which translated into . . . ?"

"Shipping containers," she stated proudly. "I discovered it when I was still living overseas. I wanted to make sure I had everything set up when I returned to the States, so I did the research, found the property, and worked with a designer to create the perfect place to live. It's got everything I need, including a shooting range downstairs."

His mouth fell open. "You have a shooting range downstairs? Where, exactly?"

"I've got two containers underground I use as a range and additional storage." She looked around the bedroom. "There's a total of six forty-foot containers and two twenty-foot containers that make up my house."

"That's gotta be handy as hell, having your own shooting range on-site." He chuckled.

"It really is." She smiled. "You can come by and use it sometime."

"Thank you, I will." He paused. "Tell me about the security."

"Standard, especially in my line of work." She grinned. "But I know you understand what I mean, what with your background."

"Looked into me, did you?" He grinned, staring into her beautiful eyes. "Staff Sergeant Finn Dennis. I was in for eight years and ended up stationed here at Fort Moore as a Ranger. When I wanted to get out, I decided to stay in the area and open up my own garage."

"And the name *Denner*?"

"It's just what everybody has always called me. It set me apart from my dad." He paused, studying her face, knowing she was hesitating to ask. "My parents are retired in Florida, which doesn't really mean the same as it does for everybody else, considering that's where we're all from."

"Florida is nice. So much culture." She could tell he was dying to ask. "So, why a bounty hunter?"

He chuckled. "You read minds too?"

"Yes and no."

"So . . . ?"

She looked away, staring across the room as her body stiffened a little. "I need a shower." She pivoted on the bed slightly.

He reached over and caressed her back. "Talk to me."

"I had a lot of anger after learning about what happened to my parents, especially who was behind it." Her shoulders fell forward, and she sighed.

"That's understandable."

"There was a man who worked on the Daniels' farm, and he helped me learn how to control and channel my anger and rage." She rotated around to look at him. "Chu Long is just as responsible for saving my life as Emma. I'm not sure who I would've become without him."

"But a *bounty hunter*? I mean, it can be dangerous, right?"

"*Seriously?*" She stood suddenly and moved away from the bed.

He remained silent, giving her a moment when he realized he may have accidentally asked the wrong question.

She turned, walking back over to the bed with her hands on her hips. "Let's just say beating the *shit* out of lowlifes, wife beaters, child molesters, and anybody who abuses animals seems to give me that warm fuzzy feeling I lost out on when my parents were murdered."

He stared at her in silence.

"Oh, and I'm really *fuckin'* good at it." She smiled, realizing she was standing there naked, with her hands on her hips.

"I don't doubt that." He winked, crossing his arms over his chest.

"I still need that shower." She turned toward the bathroom and stopped. "Join me?"

"Absolutely. You go start the water."

"Okay." She moved toward the bathroom but paused before walking in. She glanced over her shoulder. "Thanks for listening."

"Of course." He watched her walk into the bathroom, shaking his head when he heard the water flowing in the shower. *Yes, she is truly an amazing woman—and whether she believes it or not, she needs protection.*

They showered and then climbed into bed. It felt normal, like he belonged there, something Jacqui had never allowed here before. His light snoring made her laugh a little, and then she remembered the state of her brown leather jacket.

She carefully slipped out of bed and picked up his clothes, tossing them in the wash. She walked over to her personal laptop and pulled up Amazon to order another jacket.

"Hey." His whisper in the dark made her smile. "What are you doing?"

She closed the laptop and walked back over to the bed, her body lit by only a hint of moonlight shining through the windows above.

"I needed to order another leather jacket." She placed her left knee on the bed, pushing the covers away to crawl in.

"How does your wound feel?"

"Hmm, better. Thank you." She leaned over and kissed him passionately.

"My Lord, woman."

"What?"

"If this is you with an injury, a can't even imagine what you're like when you've healed." He chuckled, glancing over at her.

"Well, I have every intention of showing you." She smiled in the dark, kissing him again as she pressed herself into his warm, muscular body.

CHAPTER 13

DENNER WOKE UP AND ROLLED OVER TO FIND HIMSELF alone in bed. He looked around the room and discovered Jacqui was nowhere to be seen. He listened for a moment, picking up on music coming from downstairs—from the middle of the barn, it sounded like. He got out of bed and walked over to the double sliding barn doors. Opening the doors allowed AC/DC's "Thunderstruck" to pour in around him. He glanced down to see Jacqui doing pushups, keeping perfect time with her reps.

"Good morning," his voice boomed over the music.

She finished a rep and planted a foot, standing up. She smiled when she looked up and saw he was standing there naked.

"Well, good morning to you, too, Staff Sergeant Dennis. Sleep well?" she teased, walking over to turn the music down.

"Better than I have in I don't know how long." He grinned when he noticed her gaze traveling over his body. "You look like you're feeling much better this morning. Just be careful not to overdo it."

"I will try to behave. Are you heading out now?"

"No, I've got a minute. I asked George to open the shop this morning."

"Good, then I imagine you have time for breakfast and maybe to go over my new truck with me?"

"Sure. Hey, you mind if I grab a quick shower first?"

"Not at all. Oh, check the dryer. Your clothes are probably done." She chuckled at the surprised look on his face.

"When did you wash them?"

"Last night, before I ordered a new jacket." She winked. "See you downstairs."

He closed the doors and disappeared, and she went back into the house. She washed her hands and splashed water on her face and down her neck to cool off a bit before starting breakfast. She wasn't sure what he liked, so she stuck to the basics: coffee, eggs, bacon, and toast.

Ten minutes later he came downstairs to join her.

"You can *cook* too?" He walked over to a barstool and took a seat.

"I was raised on a farm—of course I can cook," she chirped with sass.

She set a plate down in front of him and turned to grab a mug and the coffeepot. When she turned back toward him, she noticed his eyes and a smile as he looked over the yoga pants and sports top she was wearing.

"Coffee?"

"Hmm, yes, please." He shook his head, looking down at his full plate.

"What?" She poured coffee into his mug and paused, waiting for his response.

"Is there anything you can't do?" He grinned at her.

Jacqui thought for a moment and then glanced over at the fish tank. "Apparently, I can't keep goldfish alive."

"Yeah, I was going to ask you about that."

She shrugged, nodding at his food. "Go ahead and start."

She walked over and grabbed her plate after pouring herself a cup of coffee.

They ate together, chatting about different things, and when she cleared the dishes, he helped. They loaded the dishwasher, and he couldn't help studying her. She was truly the most remarkable woman he'd ever met.

She hung the dish towel back on the handle of the dishwasher and looked up to see him watching her.

"What?"

"It's just . . ." He shook his head. "I had no idea how incredible you were."

He stepped forward, wrapping his left arm around her waist, and pulled her in for a soft kiss. He reached up, tracing her jawline with his fingertips.

She looked deeper into his warm brown eyes and knew she couldn't hide how she felt. Maybe it was time she didn't hide anymore.

"You're pretty impressive yourself, mister." Her arms slid up and encircled his neck, pulling him in for a more passionate kiss. She pulled back suddenly. "Oh, wow! I really do need a shower. Be back in fifteen minutes." She moved across the kitchen toward the stairs.

He chuckled. "I'm guessin' it's best if I wait down here?"

"Oh yeah!" she called out, racing up the stairs, smiling when she heard his laughter behind her.

WHERE IN THE WORLD DID YOU FIND A '78 K10 SILVERADO with a canopy?" Jacqui walked around the new truck, looking it over. She stopped near the front-left quarter panel.

"There was a guy in Oregon who was pretty eager to part with it, so I made him an offer. I had another car coming into the shop from California, so I just had my guy swing by and pick it up." He watched her face. "You like it?"

"Definitely."

Denner chuckled. "Good. Why don't you climb inside, and I'll tell you all about your new ride."

She opened the driver's-side door and climbed in.

He stood in the open doorway, admiring her enthusiasm.

"It's the original paint job—patinaed, like I know you wanted. The canopy I added, and of course got a little creative to weather it up for you. I had the windows tinted to help keep the heat out and offer you more privacy. The four fifty-four with airbag suspension will improve your ride, offering you more stability, especially if you have to go off road. Four-wheel drive and a turbo four hundred A/T gives you more torque, which is great since I added a winch to the front."

"Oh, this is almost as exciting as a new knife." She caressed the steering wheel as she looked around the cab.

"*Almost?* Well then, follow me, please." He stepped back and she jumped out of the truck. "I also got that bed slide installed for you." She followed him to the rear. He dropped the gate and pulled the slide out. "I've got to say, this is brilliant. Should make things easier for you."

She reached out and slid the bed back and forth a few times, smiling like a kid with a new toy.

"It's just perfect, thank you." She stepped closer and kissed him. "I can't wait to leave."

"Leave?"

"Yes, I've got a job in Atlanta." She looked at him. "Thank you so much for the incredible truck."

"You're welcome. Well, I should get going. No telling what George will do if I'm gone too long." He leaned over and dropped a soft kiss on her lips. "Have a safe trip, and call me when you get back."

"I will." She closed the tailgate. "Oh, the keys and checks." She handed him the keys to the other truck and a check in the amount of their agreed-upon price. The other check was his twenty percent. "Thanks again. Oh, and I've already cleaned out my old truck."

"When will you be back?"

Jacqui put her hands on her hips. "You keepin' tabs on me, mister?" Her coy smile was undeniable.

"After all of last night's events, *definitely*." He smiled and kissed her again. "Stay safe."

Jacqui watched Denner walk over to her old truck and climb in. She was still wrapping her mind around everything that had happened the night before. She reached down, her fingers tracing the outline of the bandage she'd decided to wear for another day. She'd gotten lucky last night, in a few ways.

She chuckled and walked back toward the house. She still needed to pack up her supplies for the recon job she had, something she still wasn't ready to share with Denner. He'd probably want to help, which would be sweet, but right now, he was still too much of a distraction to have around while on the job. She smiled to herself.

Lord, what a man.

CHAPTER 14

ALI WAS DONE WITH HIS SPECIAL RESEARCH PROJECT. Since the only thing he'd had to go on was a name, the first thing he did was delve into social media. *Nothing.*

Initially, the project was proving to be more of a challenge than he'd thought it would be, but then he simplified his search, going back to the basics.

He finally found two listings: a birth certificate and death certificate on the same day. Jacqueline Indigo DeMott was born November 10, 1999 to Victor and Savannah DeMott and died shortly after birth. At least, that's what the death certificate indicated. The problem was, there were no records of a burial or cremation for the child, which was required by law. There was no other information tied to that name anywhere.

Ali had turned his attention back to the parents and discovered Savannah was in fact his boss's sister, and Victor was his business partner years ago. Victor had been the *De* in DeWhit Holdings. The parents had both been tragically murdered just a few days after the baby was born. Ali shook his head. *Something just doesn't seem right about all this.*

When Whitlock assigned the task to him, he seemed cold and businesslike, not like someone who was concerned they might still have a living relative out there who could be in trouble. Ali hadn't detected any genuine level of concern for the girl's well-being, only an eagerness to see what could be found out about her.

Ali had managed to find the name of the young nanny, Emma Daniels, who'd been hired a year before. After the death of the DeMotts, she appeared to have moved back home with her family and, shortly thereafter, adopted a child, Jacqueline Daniels. *Coincidence?*

Again, things just felt a little off with everything he was finding. Perhaps the nanny had stolen the baby and had the parents killed; however, that wouldn't explain why a doctor had signed off on a false death certificate. Of course, that doctor was now dead, so no comment from him. *Damn.*

It appeared the child had been raised by Miss Daniels and then, at the age of seventeen, while traveling abroad, Jacqueline Daniels just disappeared. Maybe she'd been kidnapped, or randomly killed and her body was never found, which was why there were no records of her death or anything after 2017.

Ali stared down at the file he'd compiled and shook his head. Time to present his findings to Mr. Whitlock and hope the matter would be considered closed, but something in his gut told him it wasn't over.

Ali walked out of his office and opened the door to the stairwell. He ran up the stairs to the top floor and popped out just across the hall from Mr. Whitlock's office.

"Is he in?" he asked Margie.

"Yes, and he's been expecting you." Her tone told him to err on the side of caution.

He smiled and nodded his thanks.

He knocked and waited.

"Come in."

Ali opened the door and walked straight over to Whitlock's desk.

"I have that report for you, sir." He handed him the folder.

Whitlock opened it and scanned the sheets. "What the *hell* is this?"

"It's my report, sir." Ali stood still, staring at the man behind the desk.

"So this is your initial report? There's more coming, I hope."

"Sir?"

"Look . . ." Whitlock stared at Ali, attempting to impose his power. "I told you I wanted all the information on that name I gave you. This clearly isn't it."

"Sir, as far as I can tell, the young woman is dead."

"Did you find a death certificate, burial, or cremation of any kind?" Whitlock asked.

"I found a death certificate for the baby after she was born, but nothing after that."

"So that would be a *no* to a burial or cremation ceremony of any kind." Whitlock's sarcastic tone was clear: he was not satisfied.

Before Ali could respond, Whitlock turned in his chair and stood, suddenly walking over to his minibar. The silence was heavy in the air as he poured himself a scotch over ice and walked back to his desk. He took a seat and a sip, looking at Ali again, this time an unnerving calm behind his steely-blue eyes.

"Well?"

"No, sir, I didn't find anything like that. I did find the nanny who was working for the DeMotts at the time of their murder, and discovered she adopted a child after she moved back home with her family."

"*And* the name of the child?" Whitlock smirked.

"The child's name was Jacqueline Daniels." The look on Whitlock's face told Ali he was far from done with the project. In fact, the man was clearly irritated.

Whitlock looked at the young man, casually leaning back in his chair and swirling the cubes of ice around in the glass.

"You know, you are not the first IT specialist I've hired for special projects. They got me results but I knew they were not the best, so I made do." He took another sip, enjoying how nervous the young man was becoming. "But I wanted the best this time, and everything on your résumé and in your interview told me *you* were the best. Which means I expect the best results from you. Do we have an understanding?"

"Yes, sir." Ali pushed his glasses back into place. It felt like it was getting warmer in the office.

Whitlock stood and moved around his desk, stopping inches from the young man's face. Despite the fact that Ali was taller than him by at least three inches, Whitlock's demeanor was extremely imposing, even having to stare up into Ali's eyes.

"You're the best, and that's exactly what I want from you. I don't care how, but find out if that girl is still alive. Not this half-*assed shit* you just gave me." He pushed the folder into Ali's chest. "Now, get me what I asked for in the next forty-eight hours, or clean out your *fuckin'* desk. Are we clear?"

"Crystal." Ali placed his hand on the folder still being pressed into his chest. He turned and walked out the door. He glanced at his watch. *Close enough.*

"I'm gone for the day, Margie."

"I understand." Her tone was sympathetic. "Have a good night, kiddo."

"Thanks, you too."

Ali moved toward the stairwell and stopped by his office to gather additional files on his way out the door. Guess he needed to use his systems at home to go deeper into this Jacqueline person. The systems here at work simply would not cut it. That way, he could also keep whatever he found hidden from Whitlock until he determined he should really share it. It was going to be a large-pizza-beer-and-dark-web kind of night.

JACQUI SAT IN HER TRUCK, WATCHING SEVERAL EMPLOYEES for DeWhit Holdings leave for the day. She'd decided to park in a lot over from the main building, recognizing immediately when she pulled up that her truck would not blend in. It worked out because she had a clear shot of the main entrance of the building and a full view of the parking lot. Watching the people come outside, most seemed to be happy but tired from the week, probably excited the next day was Friday. Then she noticed him—a young man moving toward his car. He looked frustrated. He popped the trunk and put a bag inside, then slammed it shut. He looked around for a moment like he was concerned someone might have noticed. Jacqui did. He got in and drove off. Well, it seemed Whitlock still had the ability to piss people off. She looked down, adding to her notes, including the license plate of the angry young man. He might come in handy later.

Jacqui picked up her monocular, scanning the upper windows of the building again. According to the city plans she'd found online, Whitlock had the corner office located on the top floor on the west side of the building. She scanned across the top of the structure, discovering a man standing at the windows, gazing off across the city's skyline. She knew from all the pictures she'd found online—it was him. Her vision became blurry, and she realized unshed tears were forming in her eyes. She looked away, setting the monocular in her lap and exhaling as she felt anger rising deep within her. *Time to go.*

She started the truck and wiped any tears away that had escaped from her eyes. Tonight, she would treat herself to a nice dinner and a long bath. *One upscale hotel with great room service, coming up.*

ALI GRABBED ANOTHER BEER FROM THE REFRIGERATOR AND sat back down in front of his three monitors. He had been working for a little over three hours, using his hacking skills and taking lots of notes. It was now coming up on nine o'clock at night, and he felt like he was just getting started uncovering what the hell had really happened to the DeMotts.

He'd decided he needed to widen his search, look deeper into her parents. Start at the beginning. What he discovered made him feel even more uneasy about the man who employed him. Lionel Whitlock was not just an asshole to *him*, but perceivably to the rest of the world as well.

Whitlock's younger sister Savannah had married Victor DeMott, who then went into business with Lionel, creating the company DeWhit Holdings, which was incredibly successful, working with international companies as well as ones in the States. At one point, it looked like Whitlock had suggested a merger with a company overseas with a less-than-stellar reputation. Everything Ali was finding suggested DeMott wasn't happy with the prospect of working with them and certainly didn't want the merger to happen. In fact, it appeared DeMott was going to attempt to buy his brother-in-law out and perhaps persuade or push Whitlock out altogether.

Ali actually looked into both men's transcripts and discovered that even though Whitlock had also studied business at the University of Georgia, he seemed to have barely made it through, while DeMott had graduated with honors. Clearly he was the real brains behind the operation.

Ali flipped to a page of his notes, glancing through a few possible rabbit holes to go down. If Whitlock *had* been pushed out, there was no way he would have been nearly as successful as he had been working with DeMott. *Was Whitlock really the one who ordered the hit on his own sister and business partner?*

Ali reached for another piece of pizza and took a bite. He'd put in a call to his buddy Michael Rush, who was now working freelance for the highest bidder. He'd met Mikey at MIT and they became fast friends, bonding over who had the best hacking skills. Mikey had won, but Ali had learned a lot from him and now he was hoping Mikey could help him solve this mystery.

Ali had been researching companies for the past six years, ones that had been established but had recently changed hands. He knew Jacqueline Daniels had left the state of Georgia and then seemed to disappear, but he struggled to believe that was the end of the story. He'd found a company, Primary Ventures, purchased mid-2020 by a *J. Bleu*, which caught his eye because of the last name. Jacqueline DeMott's middle name had been *Indigo*, which was unusual. Indigo was a shade of the color blue—or more accurately, a hue. He sat back in his chair, absentmindedly chewing on the pizza slice in his hand. He glanced down at the scribbled note regarding the connection between the two words. *Now, if the phone would just . . .*

His phone started buzzing, and he smiled.

"Hello?"

"Hey, I'm surprised you're still up," the voice teased. "I thought all you corporate dudes needed your beauty sleep."

"Only if we're not already naturally pretty." Ali chuckled into the phone. "So, Mikey, what'd you find out?"

"Well, you're boss is a real piece of work. You should probably get the hell out of there as soon as possible."

"Yep, I already figured *that* shit out. I meant, what did you figure out about J. Bleu?"

"First, I must say it's nice to know the private sector hasn't completely altered your way of thinking."

"Mikey, please."

"All right, already. J. Bleu—or should I say, Jacqui Bleu—could very well be the daughter of Victor and Savannah DeMott. I'm sending you some images for your review." He paused. "Let me know when you get them."

Ali put him on speaker and leaned over his desk to open the newest email. He clicked on the zip file and opened all the images.

"Holy *shit*."

"Exactly. I used facial-recognition software and loaded up the images from the parents' DMV photos and Bleu's image to compare it, and barring actually getting a DNA test done, the probability this Jacqui Bleu is their kid is over ninety percent."

"So, she moved overseas and renamed herself." Ali couldn't take his eyes off the beautiful face with the indigo eyes staring back at him.

"I'm thinkin' she did more than that."

"What do you mean?" Ali reached for his beer.

"Well, as you know, she purchased a shelf company that was just sittin' there, Primary Ventures."

"Yeah."

"And you found some property out in Dickey, Georgia, purchased under the company name, right?"

"Yes, Mikey—please, man, some time before midnight."

"Okay, but hold on to your panties," Mikey teased.

"Will you just tell me already?"

"There were two employees listed with Primary Ventures: J. Bleu and BJ Lock. J. Bleu is a bounty hunter, a *good* one."

He paused. "Pretty damn smart being listed with only a first initial. That way, they have no idea who they're hiring. And that's not all."

"What do you mean, that's not all?" Ali absently set his beer down.

"It looks like this BJ Lock takes on specialty types of jobs, the ones involving wet work and no loose ends."

"You mean, like a contract killer?"

"Exactly, and I'm pretty damn sure it's the same person. Do you understand what I'm sayin'?"

A moment of silence fell over the conversation.

"Ali, Jacqui Bleu *is* BJ Lock. She was smart creating two separate identities, considering the latter of the two is frowned upon."

Ali continued staring at the image of the beautiful woman on the screen, struggling to wrap his head around everything.

"Ali, buddy, you still there?"

"I am. Hey, how do you know BJ Lock is her?"

"Oh, I had to go deep."

"Meaning?"

"Financial records." Mikey chuckled. "They always think they're so smart, but the Mikester always finds their secrets."

"Dude!"

"*What?*"

"Look, I appreciate everything you've found for me, but remember, messin' around with banks is a federal offense, especially across state lines."

"I know, I know. I was just taking a peek, nothing more."

"Just be careful—and thanks, Mikey."

"Hey, anything for you. Just do me a favor."

"What's that?" Ali started scribbling down a new note.

"Be careful with this chick. I don't want anything bad to happen to you."

"You gettin' soft on me, man?" Ali joked.

"I'm serious."

"Well, she's not the one I'm worried about," Ali stated.

"You mean Whitlock?"

"Yeah, Whitlock. Everything I found on him points to a strong possibility he had his own sister and brother-in-law killed over a business disagreement. That's just wrong."

"Agreed. So, what are you going to do with this information?" Mike asked.

"Well, first off, I'm sure as hell not going to share it with Whitlock. I *am* going to see if I can actually give her a heads-up." Ali took another drink from his beer. "And second, I'm also quitting my job—or at least will agree to be fired."

"How exactly do you 'agree to be fired'?"

"By already having my desk cleared out before handing Whitlock a bogus report."

"Right on." Mikey laughed. "Hey, you know, if this Whitlock really means business, he's not just gonna stop with your bogus report. He's going to shop for someone else to find this girl."

"True. You know, she lost her parents when she was only a few days old because of him, her own uncle. I guess you could say despite the fact she's a serious badass, I still feel the need to protect her. It's the least I can do."

"Always the gentleman." Mikey chuckled. "I always admired that about you. Let me know where you land when it's all over. Maybe I can come visit you, just like old times."

"You got it. Thanks, Mikey."

"Later."

The call ended, and Ali looked back at his screen and smiled. Beautiful, deadly, and intelligent. *Most impressive.* He closed the pizza box and carried it, along with the empty beer bottles, to the kitchen. He had another twenty-four hours before he had to hand in his report. He would use that time to review his escape route. He knew Mikey was right: Whitlock wasn't gonna stop until he knew for sure his niece was dead. He shook his head. *What an asshole.*

Ali thought about creating a false trail in a report to hand into Whitlock and then decided to go another way. He'd also decided to send Margie an email to let Whitlock know that he was working from home on the "special assignment." He then spent the next hour looking into the lawyer friend of Victor DeMott to see if he could offer any additional information. It was coming up on 2:00 a.m. by the time he fell into bed.

CHAPTER 15

ALI STOOD NERVOUSLY ON THE DOORSTEP AFTER HE RANG the bell. The man who opened the door reminded him of a southern gentleman, with warm brown eyes, a salt-and-pepper beard, and graying hair at his temples.

"Can I help you?" His voice was polite and soothing.

"Yes, sir. Are you Anderson Steele?" Ali made sure he looked the man in the eye.

"Yes, I am."

"My name is Ali Habibi, and I need to speak with you about Jacqueline DeMott—I mean, sorry, Jacqui Bleu."

"I'm afraid I do not know of whom you speak." Steele's posture stiffened, and he started to close the door.

"Mr. Steele, please." Ali placed his hand on the door to stop it. "It's about her uncle Lionel Whitlock. I believe it's a matter of life and death."

"Oh no." Steele shook his head. "He's found her, hasn't he?"

"No, not yet, but I'm afraid it's only a matter of time. Please, sir."

"Come in." Steele opened the door wider.

Ali stepped inside and stood, waiting nervously.

Steele closed the door, expelling a heavy sigh from his chest.

"My wife is out shopping." He smiled. "We can speak in my study."

He led the way and Ali followed him through the living room, moving past the elegant furnishings and into an office on the back side of the house. Steele took a seat behind a mahogany desk and gestured to a side chair across from him.

"Please, have a seat."

Ali took a seat, unsure of where to start. He knew Steele had practiced law for many years and was busy sizing him up, which was fine with him. He knew the conversation was going to be unusual.

"So, how do you know Lionel Whitlock?" Steele leaned back in his chair, studying the young man across from him.

"Unfortunately, I work for him—at least, I do for the next forty-eight hours, give or take." Ali was suddenly very nervous. He sighed and dove in. "Mr. Whitlock hired me about six months ago as his IT specialist. A few days ago, he gave me an envelope with nothing but a name inside: Jacqueline Indigo DeMott. He asked me to find out if she was alive."

"And what have you learned?" Steele clasped his hands over his midsection.

"I learned Jacqueline DeMott had died shortly after her birth, according to the death certificate that was signed by the doctor, but there was no burial or cremation—which, as you know, is required by law." He studied the man behind the desk, recognizing admiration behind his eyes, yet he remained silent.

"Mr. Steele, we both want the same thing here. We both want to protect the young woman who is no longer Jacqueline DeMott, nor is she Jacqueline Daniels. She is a bounty hunter who goes by the name J. Bleu, and I'm concerned about what her deranged uncle will do if he finds out she is still alive. Now, I've never met her, but I don't want that to happen, do you? Hasn't she lost enough?"

"What makes you think I care what happens to her?" Steele asked, his demeanor unchanged.

Ali realized he had become more emotional than he had intended. Suddenly, his admiration for Steele was immense, recognizing he was protecting her by remaining stoic.

"Because you were Victor DeMott's best man and friends with him for four years in college at Georgia Tech." He smiled. "I'm sorry for blurting all that out; it's just the clock is ticking. I will be turning in a bogus report I know will not appease Whitlock, and then he will hire someone else to find her. When he does find her, I would bet money he intends to kill her."

Steele leaned forward on his desk. "You know, if the tech thing doesn't work out, I think you would do well as a lawyer." He grinned. "You're very thorough."

"Thank you, sir. Truth be told, as soon as I speak with Jacqui, I'm out of here." Ali looked down at his lap, shaking his head. "If Whitlock was willing to kill off his own sister and brother-in-law over a business deal, he wouldn't think twice about killing me."

"So, you know where she lives?"

"Yes, I do. I found everything there is to know about her, and if *I* can find it, so can another hacker."

"What exactly are you going to say to her?"

"Well, I think first I'm going to ask her not to kill me." Ali laughed nervously. "Then I thought I would give her all the information I'd found for the report that was supposed to go to Whitlock. I just know I feel very strongly about keeping her safe."

Steele chuckled, confusing Ali for a moment. "Trust me when I say that young lady will be the one taking care of business, but just in case, please *do* give her whatever information you can." He shook his head, staring off across the room. "You know, she came to see me herself recently. She was a perfect blend of her parents. She had her father's strong gaze yet a softness that reminded me of her mother when she relaxed. Her dark-auburn hair and those eyes, literally the color of indigo. She is truly beautiful—and yes, I agree, we need to keep her that way, keep her safe."

"That's exactly how I feel. I know it sounds strange since I've never met her, but there was something behind her eyes, even in her DMV photo, that just grabbed me."

"Feelin' a bit smitten are we?" Steele teased.

"Oh, I just . . ." Ali dropped his eyes, slightly embarrassed.

"It's okay, son. I'm sure there have been many men who were taken with her beauty and then surprised when they learned she was much more than a pretty face. You know, her mother was quite the dancer and her father was a damn-fine ball player." Steele sat back in his chair. "After meeting her, I can only imagine what she can do. She told me she was looking into her uncle."

"Well, according to the intel my buddy found for me, I don't think Whitlock has got a chance in hell if she finds him," Ali stated. "I guess that's why I want to give her the information I have on him to give her any edge I can."

"So, when are you going to see her?" Steele sat back in his chair.

"I'm turning the bogus report in on Monday morning." He sighed. "I figure I'd drive out there after, and then I'm getting the hell out of dodge."

"I can't say I blame you. I told Jacqui to let me know if she needed anything."

"Well, Mr. Steele, I should get going." Ali stood. "I've got a few more things to wrap up before I disappear."

Steele stood. "I'll show you out."

He walked around his desk, and Ali followed him to the door.

"I really do hope everything works out for Ms. Bleu." Ali stepped out and turned to face Steele.

"Oh, I believe that girl is going to be just fine." He chuckled. "I can't say I feel the same for Whitlock."

"Thank you, sir." Ali reached out and shook the older man's hand.

"Thank you for coming by. Take care."

Ali walked to his car and got in. He drove back to his apartment to finish packing.

CHAPTER 16

JACQUI GOT BACK INTO TOWN THE NEXT DAY AROUND FOUR thirty, and she was really enjoying her new truck. It was nice. Denner had done a great job, and the slide-out bed in the back was going to be a dream for the next bounty job she had. It worked well for everything. She'd called and left him and message letting him know she was back in town and running errands before heading home.

She always enjoyed the drive, especially on a nice day. Driving on Highway 37, with farmland on both sides of the road, was always relaxing for her. Well, farmlands, cemeteries, and churches. Talk about a balance. *Grow things there and bury dead things over there and pray whenever you feel like it.*

She chuckled to herself. Either way, it gave her time to think, which was good if she had a project or upcoming job. Not so much if there was nothing other than the road for her to focus on. But that's where the kick-ass sound system came in handy. Her mind went to Denner, and she found herself smiling. She reached down and pressed lightly on her injured area, which was healing up nicely. He really was an impressive man and made her feel safe for the first time in her life. His gorgeous face, with his warm, kind eyes, and a touch so gentle . . .

She felt butterflies in her stomach as a blush filled her cheeks, and she knew it wasn't because of the warm day. She'd not been with that many men, just a short relationship here and there while she'd learned any skill with weapons or fighting she thought would serve her later. They'd served a purpose, and when they got too clingy, she moved on. Well, there was that one guy who betrayed her once. She shook her head as if to move past the memory. Getting too close and letting someone in just wasn't something she'd ever really considered doing again, until now.

Jacqui decided to stop off at the liquor store before heading home. She always tried to keep stock of whatever she might want on hand, usually beer and a good whisky. She was a simple girl in that way. She parked her truck off to the side of the road in the grassy area alongside the building. She got out and walked toward the store, when she noticed a tall, lanky young man leaning against the building. He looked about eighteen, wearing faded distressed jeans and a well-worn dark-blue T-shirt. She knew from the way he was leering at her that he was going to be trouble before he said a word.

"Hey there, sexy little lady. How's about you grab us something to drink and then I show you a good time?"

"No thanks, Junior Mint. I'm good."

He pushed himself away from the building, blocking her path to the door. "Oh, come on, now. I promise you'll have a *real* good time." He stared down at her face and licked his lips. "I'll bet you *taste* as good as you *look*."

"Please move aside." She stared up into his eyes, fighting her primal urge to move him herself.

He held up his arms and smirked before moving off to the right. She walked by, and as she entered the store, she could hear his lewd comments.

"*Damn*, that's a fine ass. I'd love to split it open for ya."

Jacqui shook her head, moving farther into the store. She noticed Eddie, the owner, behind the counter, stocking supplies. He glanced over from his project, a concerned look on his face.

Eddie was good people, in his late thirties and fairly athletic. She'd gotten to know him a bit over the years. One of the most interesting things about him was he'd played in the minors for a few years before messing up one of his knees. Painkillers and alcohol took over his life for a few years and he had to retire, which caused him to really evaluate what direction he was heading. He got help and got clean, buying the liquor store shortly thereafter. Eddie had told Jacqui once it was the best way for him to stay on the straight and narrow, observing on a daily basis the effects alcohol could have on people. Turned out, he had saved a few lives other than just his own over the years.

"Everything okay, Jacqui?"

"Hey, Eddie. Yeah, just a minor outside, looking to score a drink." She pulled a six-pack from the refrigerator and carried it up to the counter.

"Sounded like he wanted to score more than booze." Eddie shook his head. "Sorry you had to deal with that."

"It's fine. Just something too many of us seem to have to deal with these days, but nothing I can't handle—thanks." She smiled. "Can I get a bottle of Glen and a Johnnie Black, please?"

"You got it."

Eddie pulled what she'd requested down from the shelves behind the counter and carefully put them into a sturdy bag with handles. He placed the six-pack in a separate bag. She handed him cash to cover the purchase and collected the items, carrying both bags in her right hand.

"Have a good night, Eddie."

"You, too, Jacqui."

She walked out the door, not at all surprised to see the same little shit waiting for her.

"Hey, what'd you get?" He stepped in front of her, grinning at the irritated look on her face. "Come on, now. I just really want a *taste*." He flicked his tongue in her face, making a slurping noise at the same time. "So sweet and *wet*."

"Please move."

He sneered and slid back toward the building, and when she walked by, he grabbed her ass. She turned, setting her bags down carefully before punching him in the mouth with a quick left jab. Stunned, he lunged forward, and she delivered a quick round kick to his midsection with her right leg, feeling a slight twinge of pain from her injury. She quickly moved around him and grabbed his right arm, bending it at the elbow and pulling it up behind his back. She applied pressure to the back of his hand, forcing it to stay in a chicken wing.

"Now, apologize and today's lesson will be done."

"No way, you *crazy bitch*. You can't do this to me."

"Sure I can."

Jacqui applied a little more pressure until his wrist gave way and the bones broke. She let go and stepped back as the young man cried out in pain. He held his arm tightly to his body, his face distorted in pain and anger.

"Oh, man, I was just having fun. What's your problem?"

"You wouldn't take no for an answer and you were being disrespectful."

"But you broke—"

"Look, I know you think it's okay to do everything you just did and there shouldn't be any consequences for you, but that's just not how the world works—at least, that's not how it should *fucking* work. Bottom line: when the puppy continues to poke the bear simply to amuse itself and the bear finally takes a bite out of the puppy's ass, there really shouldn't be any confusion as to why."

"What? What the hell are you sayin'?"

"Keep your *fuckin'* hands off people, especially women when they've asked you not to touch them. No means no. No is a complete response. Got it?"

"Yes, *God, sorry.* I'm sorry." His face was red, still twisted in pain.

Jacqui backed up and picked up her bags, walking past the guy back toward the store. She walked in and smiled.

"Ambulance?" Eddie asked.

"Yeah, unless you want to drive him." She smirked.

"*Damn it*, girl. How many times are you gonna do this?" He reached for the phone.

"Until examples like this become so well known that ass-holes will stop randomly laying hands on women who have told them no." She grinned. "Hey, maybe before his ride gets here, take a picture of him as the poster child for consequences."

He fought a chuckle, shaking his head. "Well, now, *there's* a thought."

"Later." She smiled and walked out, moving toward the young man still holding his arm. "Ambulance is on the way."

"I *really* am sorry, ma'am." His eyes were filled with pain and regret.

"Excellent. Now, spread the word that type of behavior needs to be corrected."

He nodded, leaning into the wall more as she walked by.

She walked to her truck and loaded everything in the floorboard on the passenger side. She climbed in and drove to her favorite Mexican restaurant to pick up her order.

CHAPTER 17

JACQUI ARRIVED HOME ABOUT FORTY MINUTES LATER, feeling a flutter in her stomach when she saw a sexy Denner sitting sideways on his Harley just outside her gate. She couldn't help but smile as she rolled the window down on her truck.

"Hey, there." He slid off his bike and headed over to her.

"Everything okay?" she asked.

"Yeah. I just wanted to see how the new truck was working out for you."

He leaned in on the ledge of the window, and her pulse quickened.

"It's great, thanks. I know the bed slide I had you install will be extremely handy, and I can't wait to use it."

"Well, good. I'm glad." He smiled, reaching behind his back. "I've got a check for you from the sale of the other truck."

He handed her a check, and when his fingers brushed hers, a familiar warmth spread throughout her body.

"Thanks." She took it and tucked it into the front pocket of her jeans, not bothering to look at it.

"How's your wound?" He stared into her eyes.

"Coming along, although I might need you to take a look at it."

"Did something happen?" He leaned in farther.

"I had to teach a lesson outside the liquor store." She chuckled a little. "I probably should have left out the round kick."

"Bleu." He shook his head and laughed hard. "Yeah, I can take a look at it."

"Good. Shall we?"

"Actually, I do have another agenda for being here."

"Really? And what might that be?" Her tone was coy, and her stomach did a flip.

"I was wondering about using your gun range. I mean, you said I could use it sometime." He looked at her sheepishly.

"Yes, you can use it." She laughed. "Let's eat first. I've got Mexican, if you're hungry?"

"I am, as a matter of fact." He nodded.

"Good. Follow me." She started rolling up her window.

"Yes, ma'am." He strolled back over to his bike and started it up.

Jacqui opened the gate, and they both drove down the driveway and parked off to the side of the house.

Denner turned off his bike and set his helmet on the seat for a moment while he removed his saddlebags. He picked up his helmet and walked over to where Jacqui had parked.

"Nice bike." Jacqui smiled. "Heritage Classic, right?"

Denner turned and looked back at the bike, grinning. "Oh yeah."

"I like the all-black look. It's sexy." She winked and giggled when he chuckled to himself.

"Anything I can help carry?"

She gathered a few things from the floorboard on the passenger side.

"Yes, thank you." She turned and handed him a large brown bag. "This is the food."

"Smells good." He took the bag, watching her reach back into the truck for additional bags. "And what's in there?"

She pulled the bags over her shoulder and closed the door. "Booze."

"Good to know." He grinned and followed her toward the house.

He waited as she scanned her eye and hand, then followed her inside to the kitchen, setting everything down on the island.

"Do you want to eat here or watch a movie?" she asked, pulling some plates down from the cabinet.

"Here is good." He watched her and smiled when she looked at him. "Maybe we can talk."

She set the plates down in front of the barstools and turned to grab a couple of glasses, placing one next to each plate.

"What did you want to talk about?" She pulled the bottles out of the bag and set them on the counter.

"Whatever you want." His voice was soothing, something he seemed to do more with her now. Almost like he was concerned he might scare her away.

She smiled, grabbing some utensils from a drawer. "I'm sure you have specific questions about my background, so just ask me."

She walked back over, setting the utensils down before taking a seat on the other barstool.

"What happened at the store today?" He chuckled when she smiled and shook her head.

"Just standard bullshit I've been dealing with my whole life thus far—and I know I'm not the only woman whose dealt with this kind of crap."

"Like . . . ?" He waited patiently, giving her a moment.

"Like certain types of men believing it's okay to say crude things to women or lay hands on them even after they've been told no." She shook her head. "It just gets old."

She exhaled, staring out across the room like she was thinking. She glanced over at the empty fish tank and nodded. *Yep, still need to figure that out.*

"Jacqui?" He followed her gaze, looking over at the empty tank. "I've been meaning to ask: What happened to the fish?"

"I'm not sure. I think I might have forgotten to feed them or they got sick; either way, they're gone."

She looked at the containers of food and then over at him. "Let's eat."

"Okay." He reached for one of the containers and popped it open to find rice inside.

She reached for the Johnnie and held it out toward him.

"Yes, please, thank you."

She poured a couple of fingers in both their glasses before setting the bottle aside.

They added food to their plates, remaining silent for a few minutes while they ate.

"So, what did you want to talk about?"

"Where did you learn about . . ." He gestured around the room. "All this. Security, weapons, and self-defense?"

"When I turned seventeen I took some of the money my parents had left me and went out to discover the world. Chu Long had taught me how to control my emotions and how to defend myself, but I knew there was so much more I wanted to learn and I needed to learn it fast. I created a new identity and started hangin' out with anybody who was knowledgeable in weapons, security, and military tactics. I specifically befriended men who had served and who were willing to teach me whatever I wanted to know."

"Did any of them want more, like marriage?"

"A few but that's when I knew it was time to move on." She paused, reaching for the Johnnie and adding a couple more fingers to both their glasses. He could tell there was a part of the story she was leaving out, but he didn't want to push.

"Anyway, I knew I had to fill in the blanks, so to speak, so I started taking classes online to officially become a bounty hunter. I decided I wanted to start my own company, so I started doing research and stumbled across the concept of shelf companies."

"Shelf companies?"

"Yes, they were companies that were started but then nothing was done with them. They essentially just sat on a shelf. If someone decided to buy them after a few years of just sitting there, because they are already considered an established business, the waiting period for financial loans or whatever can actually be bypassed. I didn't need any help in that department because my parents left a lot of money to me. I liked the idea of appearing to be a longer-established company than it actually was, so when I started as a bounty hunter, whoever hired me might not take as much time vetting me. I knew I wanted to be my own boss and not have to answer to anyone." She took a sip. "If I was ever going to confront the man who murdered my parents, I needed to be ready for anything."

"You're talking about your uncle?" He took a sip.

"Yeah, I don't really like to remind myself we're related, but when I do reflect on that fact, I just find happiness again, knowing someday soon I will kill him."

She picked up her glass and clinked it against his. Her smile was undeniable, causing him to chuckle.

"Okay, *that* I get. But a *bounty hunter*?"

"I figured it was the best way to keep my skills sharp, having to use them daily. It just made sense. Plus, I still struggle with anger issues from time to time."

"Obviously," he teased. "Let me take a look at your injury."

Jacqui turned on her stool and pulled her shirt up. She smiled when he hesitated, shaking his head. He reached forward, gently pressing his fingers against the skin where she'd been cut. Despite the fact it had only been three days, she was healing up nicely. He could tell it was a little tender but not too bad.

She leaned forward a little, enjoying his touch. His eyes looked up into hers and she melted. He leaned in, dropping a soft kiss on her lips. She started laughing when she felt her barstool being dragged across the floor, closing the distance between them.

"What's funny?" he asked, enjoying her laughter.

"Why don't we put the food in the refrigerator and head downstairs for a while? Then later, if you don't have anywhere else to be for the night . . ."

"Mm-hmm, yes, ma'am." His enthusiasm amused her.

He kissed her again and then grabbed the plates, walking quickly over to the sink.

They cleaned up the kitchen and put the leftovers away.

"Be right back." Jacqui ran upstairs for a moment and grabbed Black Betty and her belly holster, tucking Rosie in the back of her pants.

Denner picked up his saddlebags, glancing around the room. There were a few art pieces on the wall, but nothing was overly done. He started looking at the walls more carefully, wondering how and where they were going to get downstairs. Confused, he grinned when he heard her laughing.

"Trying to figure out how we get downstairs?"

"No." He shrugged, trying to recover.

She smirked, stopping in front of the small console table sitting on top of an area rug near the bottom of the stairs. She carefully picked up the table and moved it off to the right before setting it down. She looked over, winking at him before moving toward the fish tank. She reached into the water along the back, where there was a decorative mushroom house. She gently pushed down on one of the mushroom tops, chuckling when he stepped back a little after hearing a mechanism underneath him.

A section of the floor where the console table had been sank down slightly and then slid off to the right, creating a three-foot square opening. She smiled, watching his eyes and face light up like a small child who had just discovered a secret.

"You are by far the most fascinating woman I've ever met."

"Thank you." Jacqui pulled her hand out of the water and wiped it off on her pants. "Shall we?"

"After you."

He watched as she sat down on the floor, dropping her legs through the opening. She reached forward, grabbed the top rung on a wall ladder, and climbed down.

"Come on down."

Denner followed her lead, climbing down into the opening. He noticed a light with a red cover mounted on the wall. When he reached the bottom, he turned around, his gaze scanning the space. He noticed the breaker panel mounted on the wall for the backup generator he'd seen outside the door upstairs the first time he'd come over.

Jacqui had done a great job setting up the perfect space for short-range shooting, which was set up on the opposite side of the containers. She had storage shelves on the far wall next to a large chest freezer. There was also a medium-size table and a couple of chairs set up where she cleaned her weapons.

She smiled, noticing his reaction. "You know, you're the first person I've ever had down here."

"Really?"

She nodded. "This way."

He followed her over to a long countertop mounted between two walls. There were a few pairs of ear protection hanging on the wall, and eye protection too. There were a few shelves under the countertop down by the floor with new target papers lying on them.

"I know it's shorter than the average indoor range—but then again, my work is usually up close and personal." She smiled, pulling Rosie out from behind her back and setting her on the countertop. "I usually drive up to the Chestnut Mountain Shooting Range when I want to practice longer-range shots."

He set his saddlebag down on the counter and smiled while he was opening it.

"What?" she asked.

"I find you incredibly intriguing."

"Really?" Her interest was piqued. "And why is that?"

"Well, without sounding misogynistic, I find it refreshing to know a woman who I not only find incredibly beautiful but also is very clever and deadly."

She chuckled. "Surely you must have met some women in the military who were every bit as clever and deadly as I am."

"Maybe, but they certainly weren't as beautiful." He winked at her.

"Well, thank you, sir. Shall we?"

"Absolutely. Show me what you've got."

"Well, here we have Black Betty, muzzled. She's who I take on most contract jobs because of her size."

"Walther PPK, nice. What does she fire?"

".380."

"Okay."

"And this is Rosie, also .380." Jacqui held up her other gun.

"Sig P365." He chuckled. "You named them?"

"Oh yeah." She stepped over to a wall and retrieved a shotgun. "And this is Rickie. I just gave her a good cleaning."

"Maverick 88 Cruiser. Nice." He grinned.

"Yep. She can come in handy on special jobs." She carefully laid the shotgun on the counter. "What do *you* have?"

Denner pulled out a Sig M17 and a large case that grabbed her attention.

"I like the M17 with 9mm FMJ. It reminds me of my time as a Ranger."

"What's in the case?"

He grinned, and she could tell it was going to be good. He was like a boy showing off his favorite toy. She fought to suppress her laughter.

Denner pulled out a Desert Eagle, laughing at her wide-eyed gaze.

"Wow! Nice!" She beamed. "What'd you name it?"

"I kept it simple." He paused, amused by her intrigue. "BFG."

She laughed. "Well, *that* works."

They loaded their weapons, and for the next hour, they practiced shooting, running drills for speed on reloading and changing over to a different weapon. Denner was impressed, admiring how well Jacqui handled the weapons, including her speed and accuracy.

Then they traded weapons, and Jacqui was thrilled to be able to fire the Desert Eagle. It was a hell of a gun.

Afterward, they sat at the table, cleaning their weapons and swapping stories about different experiences. They talked about different ammo and brands of knives they preferred.

"It's nice to see you were also taught to remove the serial numbers from all your weapons, especially in your line of work." Denner winked.

"Thanks." Jacqui chuckled. "You know, you can plan and plan, but sometimes, shit just happens."

"Exactly."

When they were done cleaning everything, they went back upstairs.

Jacqui walked into the kitchen and set her weapons down on the island. She noticed Denner hesitated to join her.

"Can I get you something to drink?"

"Sure, but I don't want to overstay my welcome."

He moved over to the island and set down his saddlebag.

"We can watch a movie, if you want." She grabbed the bottle of Johnnie and a couple of clean glasses.

"That sounds good." He walked toward her, then stopped a few feet from her. "Whatever you want."

She looked up into his warm brown eyes, the flutter returning to her stomach. "I want you to stay. I really like having you here."

"Me too." He reached for the glasses. "I've got these."

She smiled and led the way over to the sofa in the living room. He poured them a drink while she found a movie for them to watch. After the movie, Jacqui turned on some music for background noise and they spent the rest of the evening talking about everything from movies to music. Denner stayed the night again, and Jacqui admitted to herself it was definitely something she could get used to.

CHAPTER 18

ALI CAME IN EARLY AND CLEANED OUT HIS DESK. HE knew what Whitlock was going to say and had a pretty good idea how the man was going to react, and he wanted no part of it. It was coming up on nine o'clock Monday morning, and he had already moved all his things out to his car. He stared down at the folder sitting on his desk and let out a heavy sigh. *Time to just do it.*

He stood and grabbed the folder, walking briskly out of his office for the last time. He took the stairs two at a time, suddenly feeling relieved. No matter the outcome, he knew he was doing the right thing.

He popped out of the stairwell and smiled when Margie looked up from her desk.

"He's expecting you." She managed a smile.

"Thank you, Margie. I'm going to miss you." He winked and handed her a piece of paper.

She smiled and shook her head a little after glancing over it. "I'm gonna miss you, too, kiddo."

A chime came from her computer, and Ali smiled, knowing it was probably the email with a copy of his resignation he'd just handed to her.

Ali knocked and entered the office. Whitlock was sitting behind his desk and looked up, grimacing.

"You have that report for me?"

"I do."

Ali walked over and stopped in front of the man's desk. He handed him the folder, watching as Whitlock opened it and his eyes widened.

"What the hell is this *shit*?" Whitlock's chair slid back into the wall behind him.

Ali crossed his hands in front of his body, meeting the man's eye. "It's my report, Whitlock."

"This folder is empty."

"Yes it is." Ali maintained eye contact.

"Why, you little *shit*. You're fired." Whitlock tossed the folder down on his desk.

"Actually, I'm all packed up and Margie has my resignation. Do your own fuckin' dirty work, you overly important *prick*."

Whitlock glared at him. "I knew you didn't have the stones, and that's just fine. I've got someone else who is more than ready to do the job you couldn't. Now get the hell outta my office, you li'l bastard."

Ali turned and moved toward the door. He heard the man behind him grumbling insults as he picked up the receiver to make a call. Ali slowly opened the door and stepped through, pausing when he heard Whitlock on the phone.

"Yeah, call that other guy and start gathering names for a team. I want the three best hitters you've got. Once we find the little *bitch*, this ends."

Ali quietly closed the door, looked over at Margie, and grinned. "Damn, that felt good."

"Take care, Ali." Margie winked.

"Thanks. You too."

Ali moved quickly to the stairs and raced down the four flights and out into the lobby. He expected to feel a great weight to be lifted off his shoulders, not be replaced with another. He stepped out of the building, moving quickly to his car. He opened the door and got in, turning the engine over immediately, and then he sat there. *What the hell am I going to tell this woman?*

He fastened his seat belt and put the car in gear, maneuvering it out of the space and into traffic. All his belongings were already packed and in the trunk. At least, everything that meant anything to him.

This would not be his first time starting over. It would just be the first time he was actually going to disappear. Who knows? Maybe the information he was going to provide to Ms. Bleu would grant him immunity from her killing him—not that he really believed that to be an issue. As far as he knew, there was no hit out on him yet. Either way, she would be protected or at least have what she needed to protect herself from Whitlock.

Ali jumped on the highway and made the long drive out to unincorporated Dickey, Georgia. He should get there by late afternoon, as long as the traffic wasn't too bad.

J ON PHILLIPS KNOCKED ON THE DOOR.

"Come in," Whitlock said from the other side.

Phillips entered the office and walked over to the desk. His standard attire of a dark suit with a dark dress shirt underneath was always perfect for helping his athletic six-foot frame blend in anywhere; plus, it worked well for whatever job Whitlock wanted him to do. He ran a hand through his short, dark-brown hair, waiting for Whitlock to finish up a call.

Whitlock hung up the phone and handed a piece of paper to him.

"I want these guys standing by and ready to go at a moment's notice."

"Yes, sir."

"I put out some feelers and should be hearing back from a new guy this afternoon. He's supposed to be the best, but we'll see." Whitlock looked up at Phillips. "I'll call you with a name. That's all for now."

"Yes, sir."

Phillips turned, heading for the door, and Whitlock watched him leave. Phillips was a man of few words and he was costing Whitlock a pretty penny, but so far he was more than worth it. He'd found Phillips from an underground source and agreed to pay him whatever he wanted based solely on his professional reputation. At least, as much of a reputation as you can have working as special ops. So far, Whitlock had not been disappointed. He just wanted everything wrapped up. He'd spent the past twenty-three years wondering if she was still alive and if somehow everything he'd orchestrated was going to be undone. He was determined not to let that happen. He would find out soon if she were still alive, and then she would be dealt with, as well as anyone else who might know what had occurred all those years ago.

CHAPTER 19

IT WAS MONDAY AFTERNOON, AND DENNER WAS BACK OUT AT Jacqui's. He couldn't believe how close they had become in the past few days; except for a day here and there, they'd become inseparable.

Denner adjusted his ear protection again while Jacqui emptied another mag. He smiled, watching her reload, admiring her stance: very little movement when dropping an empty and loading a new one, then firing accurately again at the target. He was also impressed with the way she moved between her two weapons without hesitation, again maintaining precision while hitting the target. She fired the last shot, setting the empty weapon down on the ledge in front of her. Whoever had trained her had done a hell of a job, or she was a great student. Either way, it was a thing of beauty to watch.

They both removed their ear protection, staring down at the targets.

"Nice headshots." He chuckled as she studied the targets.

"Thanks." She laughed. "You too."

"You hungry?" He studied her face, knowing the answer when she grinned, shaking her head.

"I've got some leftovers, if you're interested."

"Why can't I take you to dinner?" He leaned against the wall, resting his left arm on the countertop in front of him.

"We've shared a meal before. What's the big deal about taking me out?"

"You tell me?" He cocked his head and winked at her.

She rolled her eyes and reloaded Rosie. She glanced at him again, reaching for her ear protection, when she noticed the red light flashing over on the wall.

"Someone's at the gate."

She holstered Rosie and walked past him toward the ladder.

"Are you expecting anyone?" Denner quickly reloaded his own weapon and tucked it in the back of his pants.

"I'm *never* expecting anyone."

He followed her up the ladder and into the kitchen. She walked to the fish tank, pausing to reach inside and turn the top of the mushroom to close the hidden door. She wiped her hand off on her pants, approaching the intercom mounted on the wall. She glanced at the camera and saw a young man in a suit—just over six feet tall, with dark hair and glasses—standing outside his car. He looked nervous.

Jacqui smiled, recognizing him. She looked at Denner, who shrugged.

She pushed the button on the side of the intercom. "Can I help you?"

"Hello, Ms. Bleu. My name is Ali Habibi, and I really need to speak with you."

"So, speak."

"Really? Here?" He looked around and then back into the camera. "I was hoping to speak with you face-to-face."

"Take off your clothes." She glanced over at Denner, who was standing by the island, and chuckled at the confused look on his face.

"I'm sorry, *what*?" Ali adjusted his tie. "You, um . . . you want me to take off my clothes? *Why*?"

"I need to see if you're armed."

"Oh, I'm not." He laughed a little.

No response from the intercom.

"Um, well, okay." He removed his coat and loosened his tie, tossing them through the open window of his car. He started unbuttoning his shirt when he heard laughter. He stared into the camera and smiled. "You were kidding, right?"

"Maybe a little. Who are you, exactly?"

He stepped closer to the camera, sighing as his smile disappeared. "Ms. Bleu, I need to speak with you about Lionel Whitlock. I have information you might find helpful."

Jacqui glanced at Denner and then back at the camera.

"Come on up."

She pushed the button to unlock the gate, watching as the man scrambled to get back in his car and drive up to the house.

"You think he's legit?" Denner walked over to her.

"That, or he's a great actor." She chuckled. "Not many people would just start taking off their clothes when asked by someone they don't know. He's genuinely nervous; besides, I recognize him."

"From where?"

"When I was in Atlanta, I was checking out DeWhit Holdings. I saw him come out of the building on his way to his car. He seemed rather upset, so naturally, I was intrigued. Besides, it can't hurt to hear what he has to say, right?" She winked, a coy smile on her face.

Denner grinned. "You've got a wicked sense of humor."

"You like it?"

"Absolutely."

She moved toward the door, and he followed her out, walking around to the front of the house. Ali's car slowly approached and then stopped a few feet from them. Denner pulled his weapon, holding it down tightly against his right leg.

The young man got out and closed his door behind him. He stood still for a moment, staring at the beautiful woman he'd only seen in a picture, which didn't seem to do her justice. His gaze shifted to the rather sizable man beside her. *Is he her bodyguard?*

"What information do you have?" Jacqui asked.

Ali laughed nervously. "I was hoping we could speak inside. It was a long drive, and I would appreciate the use of your bathroom."

Jacqui pulled her weapon and pointed it at him.

"Whoa! Hey, wait!" Instinctively, Ali put his hands up.

"Search him," she said.

Denner tucked his weapon in the back of his pants and walked toward him. Ali stood still while the muscular man's hands traveled all over his torso and down each leg, including his groin area from behind.

"Whoa! Excuse me, mister!" Ali jumped away from him. "Wow! Okay, I don't even know your name."

"It's Denner." He chuckled, stepping away from Ali. "He's clean."

Jacqui couldn't help but laugh at his efficiency.

"Felt left out of the fun, did ya?"

"Hey, just being thorough."

"Let's go inside." Jacqui smirked at Ali before putting her gun away.

She turned and walked around the corner of the building and opened the door, stepping inside. Ali followed her, with Denner coming in behind him.

"The bathroom is over there." She pointed to a door across from the stairs, on the other side of the living room.

"Thank you." Ali smiled, moving toward the bathroom. Once inside, he relieved himself and washed his hands. He stared into the mirror, trying to regain his composure.

"What do you think he's going to tell you?" Denner whispered.

"Honestly, I'm not sure. I have an idea, though."

The door opened and Ali stepped out, still looking uneasy.

"Would you like something to drink?" Jacqui asked.

"Sure. Thank you."

"Have a seat." She gestured to the sitting area.

She pulled three glasses from the cabinet and grabbed the bottle of Johnnie, walking over to join them. "So, tell me about Whitlock."

She poured a couple of fingers into all the glasses and set the bottle down on the coffee table before sitting on the sofa.

Denner picked up two of the glasses, handing one of them to Ali, who immediately downed the contents. Denner and Jacqui exchanged a look.

Ali held on to his empty glass. "First of all, I want to thank you for not killing me. I'd told Mr. Steele it was a concern of mine."

"Wait, how do you know Steele?" She slid forward on the sofa.

Ali stared at her, a genuine look of concern on his face. "I used to work for Lionel Whitlock, who it turns out is not a nice man or a decent human being, for that matter. He called me into his office about a week ago and gave me an envelope with the name Jacqueline Indigo DeMott inside. In fact, that was the only thing inside the envelope, and my instructions were very clear. He wanted me to find out as much information about you as possible, and he gave me forty-eight hours to do it. As soon as I started digging, I realized his intentions towards you were not good."

"I've actually seen you before, outside DeWhit Holdings." She slid back on the sofa. "You looked upset, and I figured you were probably working for Whitlock."

"Well, like I said, I *did* work for him, but I just quit. I wanted to buy myself some more time, though, so I could take care of a few things."

"And what exactly did you need to take care of?" she asked.

"I called a friend of mine, who helped me figure out your new identity, which then helped me locate you. It also gave me time to track down Mr. Steele and get some more background about Whitlock. I did all my research at home so it couldn't be tracked, but on my way out of his office this morning, I overheard him on the phone hiring another person to look for you, and he wanted three of the best hitters as soon as possible." Ali paused, glancing back and forth between Jacqui and Denner. "Ms. Bleu, I'm so sorry to tell you this, but when Whitlock learns you're still alive, he's going to rectify what he perceives to be a future problem."

Jacqui took a sip and set her glass on the coffee table. "How long did it take you to find me?"

"After I spoke with my buddy, who's a better hacker than I am, less than twenty-four hours." Ali glanced between them. "I'm so sorry. None of the information I found was given to Whitlock. I have the file I put together in my car, and I would like you to have it."

"So, what did you give him this morning?" Jacqui asked.

"Nothing. I mean, I literally gave him an empty folder, which *really* pissed him off." Ali grinned. "Of course, I'd already turned in my resignation before walking into his office, so I had the last laugh when he told me I was fired."

She smirked. "I can appreciate that."

"Ms. Bleu, you should know Whitlock will or has already found someone to do what I refused to do. There are others who do not believe the way I do. They have no scruples and will do just about anything if the price is right. My buddy who helped me is very good at finding information, and fast. There are others like him who may be even faster. Please be careful."

"I will, thank you."

"What are you going to do now?" Denner asked him.

"Everything I need is in my car. I'm going to disappear."

"I really appreciate you coming all the way out here to give me a heads-up," Jacqui stated. "Is there anything I can do for you?"

"No, Ms. Bleu." Ali looked down for a moment. "After learning about everything that happened to your family and what you went through, I just wanted to give you the opportunity to get him before he gets you. It seems the man will stop at nothing."

"I appreciate that, thanks." She smiled at him.

"I should get going." Ali stood. "I'll grab that file from my trunk. Thank you again for the drink and for not killing me."

Jacqui chuckled. "That's not really how I operate, but I understand what you mean. I'll walk you out."

She stood and they both moved toward the door. She felt the young man relax more once they were out of the house. It made her feel good to know Denner's presence could be so intimidating.

Ali hit the button on his key fob and opened his trunk. He pulled a thick folder out and handed it to Jacqui.

"Here. It's everything I found on you, your family, and Whitlock. There's also the business history for DeWhit Holdings and personal emails and other files off Whitlock's computer." He sighed. "Hopefully, there's something there that will help you."

"Wow, this is great, thanks." She admired the thickness of the file. "I wasn't expecting all this."

"I also included my phone number. If there is anything you need in the way of *special skills*, I would be more than happy to assist you." Ali smiled.

She smiled back at him. "Thanks, and I promise to call if something comes up. Oh, and it's Jacqui." She extended her arm, and he shook her hand. "Take care."

"You too."

Ali got in his car and Jacqui headed inside. She watched, and when he reached the gate, she hit the button and he drove out onto the main road.

CHAPTER 20

T HE PHONE ON HIS DESK BUZZED, AND WHITLOCK HIT the answer button. "Yeah."

"I have a Mr. Knox here to see you," Margie's voice announced.

"Send him in." Whitlock stood and buttoned his suit jacket.

He stepped out from behind his desk and waited. The door opened and a tall, lanky man around the age of thirty entered. He was wearing a lightweight black jacket over a gray T-shirt and a gray newsboy cap with dark jeans. His eyes were shifty and deceptive, looking around the office. He looked Whitlock up and down as he approached him.

"Mr. Knox, thank you for meeting with me." Whitlock extended his arm, and the man reluctantly shook his hand.

"It's just Knox."

"All right." Whitlock smiled. "Please, have a seat so we can begin."

Whitlock walked back around his desk and sat, watching Knox glance around the office one last time before sitting in the chair across from him.

"Thank you for coming in. I understand you're very good at finding information, specifically at finding people," Whitlock stated.

"That, I am." Knox crossed his right leg over his left knee. "For the right price, I can find everything you want on a person."

"That's good to hear." Whitlock reached for an envelope and handed it to the man across the desk.

"Who are we looking for?" Knox took the envelope and opened it. "Jacqueline Indigo DeMott. So, who is she, exactly?"

"Who she is is of no consequence to you. I just need her found in the next forty-eight hours."

"Okay, I can do that." Knox stood, tucking the envelope inside his jacket. "I'll call when I have everything."

"Excellent." Whitlock walked around his desk and shook the man's hand again before walking him to the door. "I look forward to hearing from you."

Whitlock opened the door, and Knox left the office, walking around the corner toward the elevator. Whitlock stepped out of his office and watched as the elevator doors closed.

"Margie, please get Phillips on the phone for me."

"Yes, sir."

Whitlock closed the door and walked over to his minibar. He'd just set the top back on the decanter when his phone buzzed.

"I have Phillips on one for you," Margie announced through the speaker.

Whitlock carried his drink to his desk and sat, taking a sip before picking up the line.

"Phillips, I have a new assignment for you."

"Yes, sir. How can I help?"

"I just put a new guy on the Bleu project. If he's as good as his reputation, I should be able to acquire everything I need within the next forty-eight hours. He just left the office—a tall, lanky fellow in dark clothes and a cap."

"I have eyes on him as we speak."

"Excellent. Keep eyes on him until you hear from me again."

"Copy that."

Whitlock ended the call, pleased once again he had Phillips on the payroll. A few years ago, when a business merger had started going sideways, Whitlock started receiving threats, which was unusual since he was the one usually doing the threatening. Some people just didn't know when to throw in the towel and fold. Phillips never questioned his orders, and because of that, he was paid very well. The man was great for private security and special assignments. Either way, Whitlock had the utmost confidence the job was in good hands.

CHAPTER 21

HAVE KNOX HERE TO SEE YOU, SIR." MARGIE'S VOICE CAME through on Whitlock's desk phone.

"Fine. Send him in."

Whitlock glanced at his watch. It was just over twenty-four hours, and the hacker had returned, hopefully with all the information he'd been waiting for.

Knox entered the office, closing the door. He pulled a dark-blue folder out from under his arm as he walked toward Whitlock.

"Here is all the information you asked for." Knox handed him the folder.

He started to sit when he heard Whitlock clear his throat.

"Thank you. I'm going to review the contents, and if everything I need is here, I will transfer the other half of the balance into your account. Thank you for being so expedient about the job." Whitlock stared at the semi-confused Knox. "You can go now."

Knox shook his head a bit. "Later." He turned and headed toward the door, stepping out of the office and closing the door behind him.

"Margie, get Phillips on the line and then hold all my calls." He hung up without waiting for a response.

Whitlock walked around his desk and over to his minibar, pouring himself a couple of fingers of Glenfiddich. He took a seat behind his desk again when his phone buzzed.

"I've got Phillips on one," Margie stated.

He picked up the phone. "Phillips, I need you to go ahead and follow Knox. I'm going to review the information he gave me, and I'll call you back in an hour."

Whitlock hung up the phone and picked up the folder, leaning back in his chair at the same time. Time to learn who Jacqueline Indigo DeMott had become. He opened the folder, and the image of a beautiful young woman was the first thing that caught his eye. He scanned the first page and chuckled when he noticed her new name: Jacqui Bleu. Then he noticed Primary Ventures had listed the owner as J. Bleu. She was a bounty hunter and apparently also went by BJ Lock when more discreet jobs were available. Knox had even included financials showing both identities linked to Jacqui Bleu and Primary Ventures. She was clever, so it seemed, taking after her father in that regard. He glanced back at the DMV photo attached to the left side of the folder. Her beauty reminded him of Savannah.

Whitlock flipped the first page over and found a few of the individuals who had hired her in the past. *Damn, that boy was good.*

Knox had put together a very comprehensive folder full of all kinds of information that would not normally be so easy to obtain. Then again, he had no idea whom Knox had talked to or what he had to do to get the information. Not that it really mattered. Hackers by nature were fairly tight-lipped when it came to how they got things done.

He flipped to the third page, impressed for a moment there actually *was* a third page. He paused when he saw the name listed next to a complaint: Dexter Carter. Apparently, Jacqui had taken a bounty assignment for him a little while ago, and he had not been entirely satisfied with her quality of work. *Wonder why.*

Whitlock picked up the phone and dialed the number for Carter. He got the man's voicemail, so he left a message asking to be called back as soon as possible on his cell.

He reviewed the rest of the information in the file, impressed Knox had not only found the property location for what was most likely her home, but he had also located the family and their farm where she was raised. There was also a list of businesses she'd worked with for customizing her vehicles. Yes, Knox had really done some impressive work for him. He glanced at his watch and chuckled. *Too bad it was going to be his last.*

Whitlock quickly made another call.

A deep voice came through the phone. "Hello, sir."

"Phillips, do you have eyes on Knox?"

"Yes, sir."

"Please close that account as soon as possible."

"Copy that, sir."

The call ended and he sat back in his chair, thinking about the business meeting he had tomorrow in Tennessee with an old college alumni who was in desperate need of selling his company or shutting it down. They'd been emailing back and forth for months now, with Whitlock making pitches left and right about how much he was willing to pay for the company. He'd assured the man he would be retiring quite wealthy if they could agree on the terms. Finally, Whitlock had gotten the man on the phone and set up a meeting at the small out-of-state company.

Whitlock gathered everything he needed for the meeting the next day and tucked all of it into his briefcase. He would take the time to read the rest of the file on the way there, as well as figure out exactly how he was going to take care of that niece of his.

PHILLIPS HAD BEEN TRACKING KNOX ALL DAY, ALL OVER town, noting the man was not afraid to spend money. Most likely since he was counting on the balance for the job he'd just completed for Whitlock to come through any minute now. Unfortunately, that would never happen. He was amused, following his mark to a fine restaurant, an upscale bar, and then to one of the best gentlemen's clubs in Atlanta. It was nice to see a man living like it was his last night on Earth, even if he had no idea how true that was. Knox had been at the club for about an hour and a half when he decided to grab a smoke in the alley out back.

Phillips followed him out, having already surveyed the alley as a perfect place to close the account. Knox was leaning against the wall near a dumpster, enjoying his smoke, and never even turned around when the door opened behind him. Phillips clamped his left hand over the man's mouth, driving his penknife into the hollow section of the back of the head before turning the knife. Once the body went limp, Phillips left the knife in to plug the hole, using his own body to move the dead weight forward. He flipped the lid open on the dumpster and grabbed the dead man's right leg after placing his left hand under the arm. He lifted the body up and dropped it into the bin. Phillips closed the lid and walked toward the open end of the alley, pulling his gloves off and slipping them into his pocket.

He then made a call.

"Is it done?"

"Yes, sir. The account is closed."

"Thank you, Phillips." Whitlock smiled, reaching over to turn off this bedside lamp.

CHAPTER 22

WHITLOCK WAITED IMPATIENTLY IN THE LOBBY OF THE small company. It had been a long drive from Atlanta to Tennessee, and now the meeting was running late. He was anxious to get started and wrap things up so he could move on. Whitlock was not accustomed to having to wait for anything, and it tended to make him grouchy. Glancing at his watch again, his irritation grew when he realized he had still not heard back from Dexter Carter. It was coming up on one o'clock in the afternoon, and the only levity he'd felt so far in the past twenty hours was all the information on his niece he'd acquired from Knox and the fact he didn't have to pay him for the work he'd done.

Whitlock hadn't raised an eyebrow when the smug hacker demanded a payout of a million dollars for his services, half to be paid up front. He had found the hacker's demands to be a little over the top initially, but then, when he'd presented his findings in less than forty-eight hours, Whitlock was rather impressed. Of course, having Phillips close the account on Knox not only got him out of having to pay the balance of his fee but then he filed a complaint with the bank claiming he'd been hacked, so in the end, Whitlock got his money back and tied up a loose end. He chuckled and checked his watch again, pleased when the conference room door finally opened.

"Lionel Whitlock." A man walked out, offering his hand. "It's been a long time."

Whitlock stood and shook his hand. "Malcom Bennett, good to see you again after all these years."

"Please come in."

Whitlock followed the slightly shorter man into the room. He unbuttoned his jacket and took a seat at the opposite end of the conference table.

"I trust your trip here was pleasant enough." Bennett took a seat, staring across at Whitlock.

"It was, despite the long drive. I was able to get some work done on the way." Whitlock opened his leather folder. "I trust you've had time to review my offer to help save your company."

"Yes, I have, but I believe the best thing for me and my company is to fold the business, and then I'm going to retire." Bennett studied Whitlock, knowing right away he wasn't happy.

"I don't understand." Whitlock leaned forward over the table. "Was the offer I made you not enough?"

"Oh, it was plenty and then some. I just decided, after reviewing your past business dealings and your reputation, that I would rather close my doors than have even my failing business be associated with your name or reputation." Bennett leaned back in his chair and pressed his fingertips together into a steeple. "I'm sure you understand." The corners of his mouth remained in a slightly upturned position.

Whitlock picked up on the hand gesture and was furious. "What I understand is, you've wasted my time and resources—two things I place a high value on. Your disinterest in my offer could have been conveyed in a phone call."

"That's true, but then I would have missed the sheer delight of seeing such anger on your face." Bennett chuckled. "Whitlock, as far as I can tell, you are the same cheating bastard you were in college. You can lie like nobody's business, and I just don't want to be associated with you in any way, including the sale of my company to you."

"You *lousy prick*." Whitlock was on his feet, buttoning his jacket. "This is not over."

Bennett stood. "Well, for you it is. Now, get the hell out of my office."

Whitlock stormed out of the conference room and moved quickly to the elevator. He rode the car all the way down to the ground level and exited the building as quickly as possible. He couldn't believe that little bastard had no intentions of ever selling.

He sat in the back seat, stewing and staring out the window as his driver maneuvered the vehicle into traffic. He rode in silence, mulling over the bullshit decision Bennett had made. The guy had always been envious of him in college, always trying to worm his way into the group he ran with. That was fine. So Bennett didn't want to sell him his company. Whitlock would find another way to get it. His phone rang, and he pulled it from his inside pocket. He didn't recognize the number.

"Whitlock here."

A raspy voice came through the earpiece. "Lionel Whitlock?"

"Yes. Who's calling?"

"Dexter Carter, calling you back about a bounty hunter who goes by the name J. Bleu."

"I'm glad you called back. What can you tell me?"

"She's a *bitch*!" Carter yelled into the phone.

"Arw, she's a bitch," a parrot mimicked in the background.

Silence hung in the air for a moment.

"Is that all you can tell me?" Whitlock asked.

"That, and she doesn't like it when you make changes to a deal that's already in the works. She *fuckin'* shot me and then claimed another two thousand dollars for the job she did, all because I told her she could've just offed the guy, which she ended up doin' on her way out the door anyway." Carter coughed a little. "My shoulder is *still* killin' me."

"And when exactly did this happen?"

"Just over a week ago. Do you have any idea how difficult it is to get blood out of the carpet? I just had my office redone. What a *bitch*. It was probably that time of the month."

Whitlock could tell this man was just another piece of shit he was going to have to close the account on after everything was said and done. He *did* agree with his niece, though, especially after what he just went through with Bennett. Changing a deal after the ball was in motion was just bad business. Of course, speaking with this piece of trash was giving him a wonderful idea.

"Well, I'm still thinking about hiring her for a job I have coming up," Whitlock stated, looking out the window.

"You can't be serious, man—even after everything I just told you?" Carter took a long drag on his cigar.

"Yes, I'm sure."

Carter exhaled. "All right. But, hey, don't say I didn't warn ya."

"I understand." Whitlock chuckled, thinking about everything he had learned about Bleu and everything Carter had just told him.

"Oh, one last thing . . ." Carter coughed into the phone.

"What's that?"

"If you happen to meet this chick face-to-face, come heavy or bring some muscle, not that either did me any good. She put Tucker down hard. *Li'l bitch* has got some skills."

"Good to know, Carter. Thank you so much for the call-back and information."

Whitlock ended the call smiling at the thought that ran through his head. He pushed the button to lower the partition.

"Wilkens, what is our ETA back to the office?"

"We're making good time, so I would say we should be back by four this afternoon."

"Perfect."

Whitlock smiled and raised the partition back up while he made another call.

"Hello?"

"Phillips, I need you to go into my office and pull the special file Knox dropped off recently. There is someone I would like to hire for a specialty job, and I want to make sure the request goes out tonight."

"Do you want me to do the job instead, sir?"

"No, no." Whitlock chuckled. "I actually have another assignment for you. I want you to head on over to see a Dexter Carter and close the account. You'll find his location in the same file on my desk."

"Yes, sir, right away."

"Thank you, Phillips."

Whitlock ended the call and put his phone back inside his jacket. He glanced out the window and smiled. Malcom Bennett's company would be his after all. Whitlock just had to remove the current obstacles in his way.

CHAPTER 23

J ACQUI WAS ENJOYING THE EVENING BREEZE AS IT TRICKLED in from her open windows upstairs. She'd pulled another contract job off the wire and was familiarizing herself with the mark's schedule and routine. He was located in Chattanooga, Tennessee, in the Southside District, so she figured she'd leave at six the next morning and get down there around noon, which would give her plenty of time to see what foot traffic was like around the location. Then she would plan everything accordingly.

Her racing suit was clean and already in the trailer with the extra supplies, and all weapons were good to go. Including the newest edition to the family, Bianca, a Beretta .40 cal with twelve-round mag capacity. It's not that Black Betty or Rosie had ever failed her. Even Rickie, the Maverick 88 she kept tucked away on the Ducati, had served her well, but she realized sometimes a girl could use a little more power.

She'd found a great used trailer a couple of years back when she first started taking specialty jobs. She'd had Denner take a look at it to make sure it was structurally sound and had him do some custom renovations like installing cabinets and a countertop across the front wall. It was great for storage and very functional with all the necessary electrical modifications required for a small refrigerator and an extra flashlight. Water, snacks, and an ice pack were always on hand because she liked being prepared. Recent events made her double-check her first aid kit, making sure it was also well stocked.

All those little additions and conveniences were nice, but all she really cared about was protecting her baby, the Ducati, which was already loaded and secured in the trailer. Yes, the Ducati was special, which was why it was only used for the jobs demanding no loose ends. In and out.

Now she just needed to figure out something to eat.

Her phone rang, and she smiled when she saw it was Denner.

"Hello?"

"Hey, Jacqui. What are you up to?"

"Well, I'm heading out of town early tomorrow morning for a job, so I'm getting everything prepped and ready. Why, what's up?" She felt a flutter in her stomach.

"I wanted to bring you some dinner and a movie we could watch." The sound of his voice was so persuasive.

"That sounds great, but since I'm planning on hitting the road around six, I think another time would be better. Rain check?"

"That works." He sighed. "Have a safe trip."

"Thanks."

She ended the call and stared at the phone for a moment.

It was difficult telling him no, but work came first, especially this type of job. *Timing is everything.*

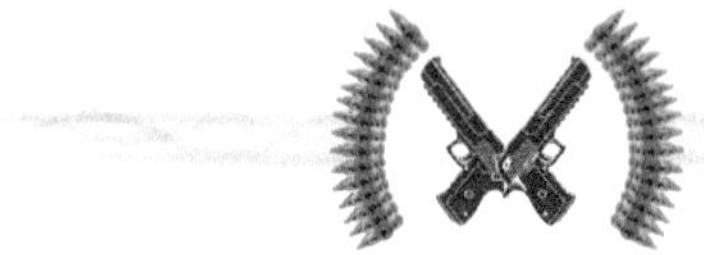

PHILLIPS SAT IN HIS BLACK SEDAN, STARING AT A BUILDING for the last hour. He'd double-checked the address, surprised it was correct. It seemed like such a shitty part of town—but then again, maybe it would offer him less chance of being interrupted. Glancing at the sky, he noticed the soft hues of pink and orange pushing through the clouds. He wanted to close the account before the parking lot and streetlights came on. He opened the car door and got out, casually walking across the street and through the parking lot toward the building. He had no idea why Dexter Carter was the mark, but for him, it didn't really matter.

Phillips had found the file Whitlock had mentioned and found the address for Carter. He'd also seen Finn Dennis listed in the people associated with the Jacqui Bleu person Whitlock was looking into. Phillips had never liked the guy, feeling Dennis—or *Denner*, as he was called—was too by the book. They'd served together back in the day, and Denner had been promoted over him after one of their missions. After that, it had just seemed like Denner rode his ass all the time, never understanding that sometimes on a job, shit just goes sideways. That didn't mean you should spend the rest of your life bemoaning that fact, nor should the answers given on your psych eval disqualify you from staying on the team. Instead, Phillips was offered a position in a different department, one that didn't allow him to do what he actually really enjoyed doing, which was killing people. That was fine. His character flaw had gotten him a sweet deal working for

Lionel Whitlock, and that prick was a mean son of a bitch. He was always sending Phillip off to close accounts, and he paid him whatever the hell he wanted. So, win-win, as far as he was concerned. He chuckled to himself. *Maybe one day soon I'll get to take out Denner.*

Phillips opened the door and entered the building, moving down the long hall toward an office in the far corner. He noticed how grimy the walls and carpeting were. The faint smell of paint could be detected the closer he got to the office, which confirmed in his own mind how much better the world would probably be minus Dexter Carter.

Phillips pulled his Sig .45 with the suppressor, holding it tight to his chest when he knocked on the door. He heard a muffled voice on the other side and watched as a large shadow was cast through the obscure glass at the top. The door opened, and Phillips put a couple of rounds into the chest and one in the head of a rather large bald man with a cast on his right arm. He stepped through the door as the large man hit the floor, moving to the left toward Dexter Carter, who was sitting behind his desk, most likely reaching for a gun in his top left-hand drawer. Phillips shot him in the left shoulder, amused when he noticed the sling the man was already wearing on his right side.

"Goddamn it, buddy! What the fuck?" Carter grunted in pain, unable to cradle his newest injury.

"Arw, what the fuck?" the parrot in the corner mimicked.

Phillips moved closer, his weapon still trained on the target. "I imagine it might be a real challenge for you to take a leak now." He smirked while making the statement.

Carter panted through the pain. "Who the *fuck* are you?"

"I'm nobody. Just here to close an account for Whitlock."

Carter's face was pale. "What? *Why?*"

"I didn't ask."

Phillips shot Carter twice in the chest and once in the head.

"Arw, why?" the parrot squawked from the corner.

Phillips turned and shot the bird. *Absolutely no witnesses.*

He put his weapon away and pulled a flask from the inside pocket of his jacket. He moved through the office, dousing any papers and both bodies. He grabbed the full wastepaper basket, scattering the trash in a trail from the desk to the door and then dousing them too. Phillips stepped over to the door and opened it. The path was clear. Moving back across the room, he pulled out a cigarette and his Zippo lighter, taking a long drag once it was lit. He reached back into his pocket and pulled out a small book of matches, lighting them up with the Zippo. Once all the matches were ablaze, he tossed the book over onto the top of the desk and turned to leave the office. He stepped just outside the door and bent down, holding the tip of his cigarette to the edge of one of the papers on the floor. He closed the door as the flames grew and spread along the trail to the desk.

Phillips moved quickly down the hall and out of the building. As he walked across the parking lot, the lights were just starting to come on. He climbed into his car and drove away just as smoke was starting to seep out from any windows in the building.

He made a call.

"Hello?"

"The Dexter Carter account is closed, sir."

"Excellent. Anything revealing left behind?"

"No, sir."

"Good. Now I need you to go ahead and send a five-man team out to a location to close an account. I'll text you the address."

"Yes, sir. How soon would you like the account closed?"

"No later than forty-eight hours."

"Consider it done, sir."

"Thank you, Phillips."

The call ended and Phillips headed to a local steak house to grab a bite to eat. He was starving.

CHAPTER 24

J ACQUI WAS ON THE ROAD BY 6:00 A.M. THE NEXT MORNING as planned, heading down I-59 N to get to Tennessee. It was a little longer of a drive, but she found it more peaceful, surrounded by lots of trees and vegetation instead of houses and buildings on either side of the interstate. It gave her time to think about her plan and also how to deal with any contingencies. Most jobs were out of state, making the trailer a necessity, not to mention doing her best to keep the Ducati out of sight where she lived. It was done up in custom fairing, in an indigo blue including additional fairing added to hide the shotgun under the seat, which usually had nothing there. All the more reason to keep it under wraps and protect her identity.

After glancing at the clock and reviewing traffic, it looked like it was going to be a pretty smooth trip. She turned up the volume on the stereo, smiling as Godsmack's "Eye of the Storm" blasted from the speakers. She settled into the drive as the scenery flew by. She needed to locate a good spot to park her rig and then scope out the area. She also needed to get into the building to set her circuit interrupter in place before nightfall.

Jacqui parked the Ducati behind some bushes as close to the building as possible. It was coming up on 8:30 p.m., and according to her intel, the mark should be on the third floor in a conference room on a Zoom call that was to end in ten minutes. There should only be two security guards on-site, so she was hoping for a quick and clean job. She tucked her monocular back in her backpack, pleased when she saw a ladder on the side of the building. She glanced around, making another perimeter sweep before moving swiftly across the parking lot to climb the stairs up to the ladder.

Jacqui pulled out her cylinder drill and drilled through the lock on the door to the roof before silently entering the building. She closed the door, remaining quiet as she slipped the drill back into her pack. She listened for a moment before moving down the stairs to the third floor. She cracked the door open and waited, pleased to hear no activity on the floor.

She checked her watch: 8:45 p.m. on the dot. She pulled Betty, looking up and down the empty hallway before stepping into the conference room. The mark looked up, his face washed with surprise and fear. Before a sound was made, she shot him twice in the chest and once in the head just under the nose. His head recoiled and his body slumped back in his chair.

Jacqui stepped back out of the room and started moving down the hall to get back to the stairwell. Two men came out of another conference room just as she opened the door to the stairs.

"Hey! Stop!"

Jacqui shot at them twice, missing on purpose. They weren't the target and had no time to pull their weapons—no sense dropping more bodies unless needed. She raced up to the top floor, closing the door quietly so it wouldn't give away her location. She immediately hit the button for the elevator. It took a moment, and when the doors opened, she hit the button to take her to the first floor. Once the doors closed, she tucked Betty inside her suit and zipped it up. Using the handrails for balance, she quickly climbed up and slid a ceiling tile aside before pushing the emergency door open and climbing up through the ceiling. She closed the door after replacing the ceiling tiles and focused on slowing her breathing while carefully balanced on the support beams on top of the car. When the car finally reached the lobby, the doors opened, and two men looked inside with their weapons drawn. Jacqui held her breath.

"Where the *hell* are they?" They stared at each other, confused.

"No idea, but we need to sweep the entire building."

Two more men appeared right outside the open doors.

"Whoever they are, they just killed Mr. Bennett, who was on a Zoom call on the third floor."

"Shit." All the men stepped in the elevator, and one of them hit the buttons for all the floors. "We'll each take a floor and search it. We need to find this person as soon as possible."

The elevator stopped at each floor, and a man got off to do a sweep. When the elevator stopped on the top floor, Jacqui waited until the last man exited the elevator and the doors closed. She dropped down into the car and pulled her weapon. She closed her eyes for a moment to quiet her mind, pushing the button to open the doors. She cautiously looked around, relieved when she saw the coast was clear. There was no time to retrieve her circuit interrupter on this job. She'd just have to cut her losses on that one. She quickly crossed the hallway, going through the door for the stairs leading to the rooftop. She came through the door, staying low and listening for any activity outside the building. She knew she needed to leave before any authorities showed up.

Jacqui climbed down the ladder and raced to the bike tucked in the bushes. She pulled her helmet on and started it up. She maneuvered it quickly out of the parking lot, hauling ass back to the truck and trailer. *That was too damn close.*

It was a five-minute ride back to her rig. She parked the bike for a moment and quickly unlocked the side door of the trailer. She dropped the rear door, pushed the bike inside, and closed the door. She secured the bike and pulled her helmet off, leaning against the rear door after locking it. Closing her eyes, she was momentarily startled when she heard a number of sirens racing past the large parking lot where she was parked.

Jacqui unzipped the jacket of her racing suit, walking to the front of the trailer. She pulled off her balaclava and tossed it on the countertop, pacing back and forth with her mind racing. She removed the suit and tucked it away in the storage unit she'd had installed. She grabbed a bottled water from the small refrigerator and took a few sips, setting it down on the countertop hard. She shook her head, removing the rest of the clothes she normally wore under her racing suit. She pulled on a black tank top, a pair of her Carhartt pants, and her brown biker boots. She put Black Betty away, replacing her with Rosie in her belly holster. Pulling on her new leather jacket, she slipped out the side door of the trailer, shutting it before quickly climbing into the front of her truck on the passenger side as another cop car flew by on their way to the crime scene. She slid over to the driver's side to start the engine, sitting for a few more moments to see if any more cops were coming by. She glanced at the clock in the truck. It was five minutes after nine. She sent a message confirming the job was done. Her device buzzed, and a sigh of relief filled the silence of the cab when she saw the payment hit her account.

Jacqui put the truck in drive, slowly moving through the parking lot, careful not to kick up any more dust than necessary. She jumped on I-24 and connected with I-75, which would allow her to make a stop to get gas, grab some food and a shower, and get some sleep. She would stop off at the Danielses' farm on the way back home. It would be good to see Emma and the rest of the family. Plus, it would be good to see Chu Long and spend time with him, maybe finish the basket she'd started last time she was there.

WHITLOCK SAT IN HIS OFFICE, SMILING WHEN HE RECEIVED the confirmation the Malcolm Bennett account was closed. He chuckled, sending the payment off to the BJ Lock account.

He almost wished he could keep his niece on for special jobs—without her knowledge, of course—but eventually she would become more of a liability. Besides, Phillips did great work.

He looked back through the information from Knox, noting all the new internet searches that had been done on DeWhit Holdings over the last week or so. She really was rather impressive, which was all the more reason to get rid of her. She was smart and, from what he could figure, very skilled at what she did. He certainly didn't need her coming for him.

A team was already on its way to the farm to take care of Emma Daniels and anyone else who'd helped raise little Jacqueline DeMott. He wanted his niece to feel the pain of losing her family before she was taken care of. Damn his sister for being clever enough to conceal the child from him. At the same time, Whitlock was impressed by Victor going to such lengths, what with having medical documents forged to hide the fact his infant daughter was still alive.

A knock on his door pulled him back to the present, and he quickly tucked all the files into the folder, then slipped it into a drawer.

"Come in." He glanced at his watch. Right on time.

The door opened and a stunning young woman entered, wearing an elegant turquoise cocktail dress and a brilliant smile. Her long, silky blonde hair shone under the overhead lights, and her golden tanned skin looked nothing short of spectacular, inviting to the touch.

"Well, good evening, my dear." Whitlock sat back in his chair, gazing at the beauty before him.

"Good evening. Ready for dinner?" Her soft husky voice stirred his loins.

She was a vision. That, combined with the great news he'd just received, put him in a festive mood.

"Absolutely, but first I feel like having a little appetizer before we go." He slid his chair back and stood, extending an arm toward her.

"Hmm, of course, sir." She took his hand, laughing when he pulled her forward. "As you wish."

He kissed her passionately and then turned her around, pressing his hand into her upper back. Instinctively, she leaned forward across the desk, stepping into a wider stance and smiling when she heard him unzip his pants. He pushed her skirt up over her round hips and ass. She closed her eyes, moaning as his fingertips pulled the thin string aside and he plunged into her. He was one of her favorite clients.

CHAPTER 25

THE NEXT MORNING, JACQUI WAS ON THE ROAD AGAIN, trying to put even more distance between her and last night's debacle. She still couldn't believe how sideways things had gone, and of course they would have been much worse had she been caught. Being seen was bad enough.

She'd spent the night at the Braselton Pilot Travel Center in a space usually reserved for an RV, but the truck and trailer were close enough, so she set up her reservation on her laptop and settled in. She'd grabbed a shower and something to eat before climbing into the back of the truck to watch a movie, setting up her simple warning system of a rope around her ankle should anyone open the tailgate.

Looking at the farmland spread out on either side of the country road was soothing for her. She pulled the truck and trailer off the road, driving down the familiar driveway where she grew up. She stopped and parked off to the side of the circular drive, glancing at the clock on the dashboard before turning the engine off. She pulled off her belly holster with

Rosie and put everything in the center console Denner had installed between the seat belt rigs. It wasn't standard on this truck, but there was just enough storage for a few weapons. She opened the driver's-side door and stepped out, laughing when she saw Copper and Rusty racing toward her. Some things never changed.

"Well, this is a nice surprise," Emma called out, walking toward her.

"I was passing through on my way back home, and I thought I would stop by." Jacqui stood up after petting the dogs. "I probably should have called first."

"Nonsense." Emma embraced her and squeezed her tightly. "Family doesn't need to call first, and you're just in time for lunch."

"Oh, that sounds good. It was a long drive."

Emma laughed, watching the dogs race back toward the house. "Let's put the dogs in the backyard and then head inside."

"Perfect."

They entered the house, chatting, and walked toward the kitchen, where Keith and Carol were preparing lunch. The kitchen had been remodeled right before Jacqui moved out with honey-spice stain on maple cabinets and a solid neutral-tone-surface countertop. It had been an expensive remodel, especially the countertop, but Carol had insisted, claiming it was easier for making pies. Keith had found that to be a compelling enough argument since his favorite kind of pie was peach.

"Jacqueline, perfect timing." Carol walked over and hugged her. "Are you hungry?"

"Yes, thank you." Jacqui looked around at all the delicious food.

"I see you drove a truck today." Keith placed the basket of homemade bread on the table, patting her on the back at the same time. "Looks different."

"Different truck. I upgraded, so to speak." Jacqui smiled at the confused look on his face.

"How do you upgrade to a '78 Chevy K10 Silverado?"

"By trickin' it out under the hood and in the bed."

They both laughed, and she knew he understood.

"Shall we?" Carol put a huge basket of fried chicken in the center of the table and wiped her hands off on her apron.

Everyone pulled out a chair and took a seat. They all held hands as Keith said grace.

"So, what brings you our way, Jacqueline?" Carol asked, passing the basket of chicken to her.

"I had an assignment in Tennessee the other day and just thought I would swing by on my way home."

"I see you've got a trailer attached." Keith added some green beans to his plate.

"I needed a few extras for the job, and the trailer allows for that. So, how have the crops been coming this season?" Jacqui reached for the bread while steering the conversation away from herself.

"Oh, pretty good so far." Keith chuckled. "Hey, do you remember one of the first times you were helping with the peanut harvest?"

"I think you were about six at the time," Carol added. "Just cute as a button."

"But not entirely aware how peanuts were fresh out of the

ground," Keith continued, laughing. "The look on your little face when you learned the peanuts had to dry out before you should eat them was priceless."

"Well, how was I to know?" Jacqui giggled. "They tasted okay, just rather *dewy* inside."

"You sure did take to riding and roping, though." Keith beamed with pride, reflecting on the memory.

"That's probably why I love riding motorcycles." Jacqui wiped her hands off on her napkin.

"Oh my, that just makes me nervous when you remind me of that." Carol leaned over and pulled her granddaughter in for a side hug. "Please tell me you're always careful."

Jacqui suddenly realized how much she'd missed the only family she'd ever known. "I promise." She dropped a kiss on Carol's cheek.

"Come on, Mom," Emma said defensively. "She's a big girl."

Jacqui glanced over at Emma, who winked at her. She had a feeling her adopted mother knew she might be into something rather dangerous, and Jacqui appreciated the support.

"Oh, I know she is." Carol pulled away from her granddaughter. "So, tell me: Is there anyone special in your life?"

Jacqui couldn't help but smile, suddenly feeling like she was seventeen again.

"There is someone I've been spending some time with, yes."

"Oh, you hear that, Keith?" She excitedly patted her husband's arm. "Hey, maybe I can take you shopping sometime, get you something a little *frillier* to wear."

Jacqui looked down at her black tank top and her dark-brown Carhartt pants, in a color *they* referred to as *sable*. That was probably as close to fancy or frilly as she wanted to get.

Not wanting to disappoint her grandmother, she just smiled. "We'll see."

"Oh, good." Carol gave her another hug.

"After we finish lunch, I would love to show you the re-modeling I had done in the barn." Keith smiled.

"I'd love to see it," Jacqui declared.

They continued their meal, reminiscing about the past and sharing thoughts about what was to come in the future. Jacqui decided she would make it a point to come visit more often.

"Can I help you with the dishes?" She stood and grabbed her empty plate from the table.

"Yes, thank you." Carol beamed at her.

They started washing the dishes while Emma cleared the rest of the table.

After everything was done, they all walked out of the house, heading toward the barn. Keith had added a few more stalls for boarding horses and two more spaces for grooming. It looked nice, and there was plenty of room to move around. Jacqui glanced down at the floor inside the barn, smiling to herself when she realized how much influence these people had had over her. The straw crunched under her boots as she moved across the floor, and she found comfort while listening to her grandfather share his experience of the remodel. She looked around the barn, noting all the maintenance equip-ment hanging on the wall in the back. Always so neat and tidy. Must be where she learned it.

Jacqui turned to see Chu Long standing outside the side door of the barn, but he wasn't smiling.

"Miss Jacqueline, it's wonderful to see you; however, I fear we have some uninvited guests arriving soon." He stepped through.

"Shit!" Jacqui whispered under her breath, although apparently not as quiet as she thought. "Sorry."

Emma and her parents were staring at her, a shocked look on their faces.

"My gun is in the truck." She walked over to Chu Long, who was now standing in the middle of the barn. "How many are there?"

"I saw only one vehicle coming down the road. A black SUV with tinted windows, so it's difficult to say how many are inside." He looked at Jacqui. "Shall we?" His smile said it all.

"Absolutely." Jacqui turned to Emma and her grandparents. "You guys head upstairs and stay out of sight."

"Well, how do you know it's coming here?" Carol innocently asked.

"Honey, when was the last time we ever saw a black SUV with tinted windows in these parts?" Keith patted her arm and winked at Jacqui. "What are you two going to do?"

"What I do best." Jacqui looked over at the wall of tools hanging nearby. "Quick, go now, and please keep your heads down."

"Come on, you two." Emma pushed her parents to head toward the stairs leading up to the loft. "Please be careful," she whispered to Jacqui on the way by.

"I will."

As Emma and her parents moved up the stairs near the side door, Chu Long and Jacqui walked over to the back wall. They both reached for a push broom, unscrewing the handle from the bristles.

"I've got the side entrance." Chu Long walked back to the open doorway and waited, pressing his body tight to the wall.

"I'll take point." She nodded at him.

They both took their places.

A man stepped through the side door, and Chu Long swept his feet, dropping him to the ground. He spun the broomstick handle like a bo staff, bringing it down and cracking the knuckles on the man's hand holding the gun. The man cried out in pain as Chu Long stepped over his body, dropping his left knee into his back when he attempted to get up. He leaned forward, placing the stick on the front of the man's throat, pulling back until his windpipe was crushed.

Chu Long stood and moved away from the man, pausing to watch his prized student at work. Unfortunately, with his attention on Jacqui, he missed the other man who slipped in, heading up the stairs right behind him into the loft.

Jacqui snapped her stick in half, doubling her weapons for the man who came through the front of the barn with his gun drawn. She stepped to the left and swung the left stick downward, knocking the gun out of his hand, and then countered with her right stick in an upward motion, striking him under his chin. He fell back, dazed.

"Hey, bitch!"

Jacqui turned and looked up to see a man standing behind Emma with a gun pointed at her head.

"You really are something to see. Beauty and brutality all rolled into a *sexy* body." He leered down at her. "Too bad I don't get a taste."

Right as he pointed the gun at Jacqui, Emma threw her head back into his nose and elbowed him in the ribs. She spun outward, away from his body, and pushed him over the edge of the loft. He hit the ground hard, and Jacqui moved forward, rolling on her right shoulder, to drive the broken stick up under his sternum just as he sat up. The man grunted, his gaze fixed on her as he gasped for air.

She stared into his wide eyes and whispered, "Not even if I was unconscious."

Jacqui stood and looked up into the loft. "Everyone okay?"

They all nodded.

She glanced at Chu Long and saw him smiling.

"Most impressive, *tre em*."

"Thanks."

She turned around and panicked when she saw the first man who'd attacked her was gone and not lying on the barn floor.

"Fuck!"

Jacqui was moving back toward the front of the barn but stopped when a large man stepped inside, wielding a huge knife in his right hand. She took a few steps back and glanced around, but she couldn't seem to locate the gun she'd knocked out of the other man's hand. She started stepping sideways to her left in a half circle as an evasive maneuver, turning her upper body away slightly.

"Hey, friend, what's say we call this a draw?" She watched the man's eyes closely.

"Hell no." He grinned, holding the knife in an ice pick grip. "I was told I get a bonus if I personally kill you. Of course, we can negotiate exactly when and what happens before that." He licked his lips, staring at her chest.

"*Geez*. You *assholes* are all alike." She slowly removed her switchblade from the front-right pocket of her pants, palming it close by the side of her leg.

He lunged forward, sweeping the blade toward her in a counterclockwise motion, missing the first time. Unfortunately, the next clockwise sweep of the blade nicked her left shoulder a bit. She hissed and jumped back to create more distance between them.

"Ooh, yeah baby." He held the blade up with her blood on it and took a long whiff. "Smells sweet. I can't wait to taste you."

"You fuckers really need some new material." She rolled her eyes, pissed off by the pain he'd inflicted.

"Get ready for me, honey."

He brought the knife up over his head, and that's when Jacqui leaped forward, driving the switchblade up into his right armpit while simultaneously grabbing his right forearm. The pain and numbness overtook him as she left her blade in and grabbed the knife from his hand. Stepping through under his arm, she bent it back and kicked the back of his knee out, dropping him to the ground. She slit his throat with his own knife, and he fell forward, dead.

She tossed the bloody knife down, glancing up into the loft to see the shocked looks on their faces.

"Oh my, Jacqueline. That was incredibly violent." Carol's

eyes were huge as she looked down at the bodies on the barn floor.

"Well, now you have a general idea of what I do." Jacqui glanced at Chu Long.

"Go." He nodded toward the front of the barn.

She turned and ran outside. The man who'd gotten away was running straight for the SUV as it barreled down the driveway toward the barn. She ran to her truck and pulled Rosie out of the center console, then stopped. It was gonna take more than her .380 to stop that SUV. She put Rosie back and grabbed Bianca, her .40 cal Beretta. Time to see what she could really do. She tucked it in the back of her pants and opened the side door on the trailer, grabbing her helmet off the countertop. She slipped it on while moving toward the rear to drop the trailer door. She jumped on the Ducati and started her up. Jacqui drove out of the trailer, planting a foot to make a hard left heading down the dirt side trail that ran to the main road. She cut across an older path to get out in front of the SUV. The Ducati popped out on the road, and she could see the vehicle heading straight for her, increasing in speed. She stopped the bike in the middle of the road and pulled out her shotgun from under the seat. She aimed at the front of the SUV, hoping to hit the hood and windshield. She fired several times, striking the vehicle, but it just kept coming. She quickly set the shotgun down and pulled out Bianca, firing the FMJ ammo several times into the front of the vehicle and hitting the radiator. The next two shots were at the driver: one in his head and the other in his left shoulder. She shot the passenger in his upper body as he instinctively reached for the wheel, trying to regain control as the vehicle slowed down.

Jacqui tucked her pistol away and grabbed the shotgun, tucking it in under her seat. She gunned the bike, moving it out of the way and clear of the SUV. The vehicle went off the road and stopped, getting stuck in a small ravine. She stared through the rear windshield at the bodies a moment longer, making sure they were not moving. Then she noticed the passenger. She dropped the kickstand down and got off the bike with Bianca in her hand, moving slowly up on the driver's side of the SUV. The passenger was just reaching for a gun when she shot him in the head through the rear door on the driver's side.

Jacqui tucked her gun in the back of her pants and walked back to her bike. She got on and rode back to the farm, maneuvering down the driveway toward her truck. She saw everyone waiting for her just outside the barn. When they heard the bike, they walked toward the trailer to meet her.

She cut the engine and removed her helmet, surveying the faces of her family. There were a few different emotions she was picking up on, and she knew after what they'd just witnessed, they would want an explanation.

"So . . ." Carol stepped forward first. "This is what you do for a living?"

Jacqui got off the bike, setting the helmet on the seat. She looked into the woman's eyes, surprised she saw no disappointment.

"Sort of." She looked down, pushing a few small rocks around with the toe of her boot. "I'm a bounty hunter, for the most part."

"And for the other part?" Keith walked over to where they were standing.

Jacqui looked up into his face, surprised to see a faint smile. "I also do specialty jobs, for the right price."

"Are the people you take down bad?" Keith asked, standing behind his wife, holding her close to the front of his body.

"Yes, they are. I'm certain I know who sent those men today. I just never thought he would involve all of you, and for that I am so sorry." She looked out across the property for a moment. "I suspect when his men don't return, he'll send more, and I need to stop that from happening."

"Well, *hell.* It's good to see you channeling all that anger you had when you were younger, and even better to know you can take care of yourself." Keith stepped forward and embraced her. He pulled back quickly, looking over at his wife. "Not that killin' isn't wrong, but I say you do them before they can do you."

"Yes, well . . ." Carol looked around at everyone. "I think I need a glass of wine. Would anyone care to join me?"

"In a little while." Jacqui looked over at Chu Long. "First, we've got some cleaning up to do. I'm going to pull the SUV out of the ravine."

She walked around them and unhooked the trailer from the truck. Then she put the Ducati away. She was just about to climb into the cab when Keith walked over.

"How many were in the SUV?" His voice was a whisper.

"Two." She looked into his eyes and was surprised when he smiled down at her.

"That's my girl. Bring the vehicle to the end of the small

path. I'm gonna make a call." He squeezed her shoulder and walked back toward the house.

"Who are you calling?" she asked.

"I've got a buddy who will come pick up the SUV, no questions asked. He's got a salvage yard just down the road."

Jacqui raised an eyebrow and smirked.

"Don't give me that look. I haven't always been who I am today. Your grandmother saved me." He winked before turning and walking away.

Jacqui chuckled and continued unhooking the trailer from the truck. She got in and drove the truck down the driveway and turned left on the main road. Thankfully, it was late afternoon, and there wasn't a lot of traffic.

She drove about a quarter mile until she saw the SUV. She slowed down, pulling in close to the rear bumper. She got out and walked to the driver's-side door, surprised when she found the door unlocked. These newer vehicles were great in that way.

She removed the keys and put the car in neutral, disengaging the parking brake and then unplugging the battery cable. She closed the door and walked back to the rear of the vehicle, chuckling when she realized it was fortuitous Denner had installed a winch on her new truck considering she never asked for it. Come to think of it, he didn't charge her for it either. That man definitely deserved something special. She smiled and hooked the vehicles together.

Jacqui pulled the vehicle from the small ravine and managed to back her truck up, pulling the other vehicle down the country road about twenty feet. She maneuvered the truck down the small path until she knew the front of the SUV was off the road. She climbed out and was dropping the tailgate when Keith walked up.

"Are the bodies still inside?" He nodded to the cab of the SUV.

"They are. I was just about to move them." She reached forward and pulled the slide out of the rear of the truck, removing a couple of tarps and a pair of gloves. She looked back at her grandfather, and she could already see the wheels turning.

"That looks handy. Put a lot of bodies in the back of your truck, do ya?"

"It's useful for moving all kinds of heavy things." She smirked and knew it was coming.

He placed a hand on her shoulder and smiled. "Don't tell your grandmother."

"It'll be our little secret."

He winked. "Let's do this." Keith grabbed another pair of gloves and slipped them on.

Jacqui stared at her grandfather for another moment, wondering what nefarious things he'd done in the past. She smiled, realizing it didn't matter, because she suddenly felt closer to him than she'd ever felt before.

They worked together, spreading a couple of tarps out on the ground and removing each body from inside the SUV. They set them on the tarp and Jacqui removed all forms of ID and jewelry before folding the plastic in and tucking it under the body. They rolled them up tight and set them in the back of the SUV. She walked back to the rear of her truck and put their personal effects in a plastic cooler in the back, slamming the gate closed.

Jacqui walked back up to the front of her truck to detach the winch from the other vehicle. Keith stood silently watching her. She wondered what he was thinking, what he thought of her now after seeing what she was capable of.

"You know, kiddo, we've all done things under the guise of good, despite others believing our actions were bad." He smiled when her eyes met his. "Your grandmother and I know how challenging your life has been, and we understand the choices you've made might not necessarily be the ones we would have made for you. But remember, no matter what, we love you and will always be here for you."

She stepped forward into his embrace, deep emotions washing over her. He kissed the top of her head and squeezed her tighter against his body.

"Come on, let's head back to the house." He patted her arm.

"Shouldn't we wait for your friend?" She looked up into his face and then at the road when she saw a tow truck approaching. "Damn, that was fast."

"Wait here."

The tow truck slowed and stopped just passed the front of the SUV. Keith walked toward the road while Jacqui walked over to the driver's side of her truck. The driver got out and extended his arm to shake Keith's hand. She realized that although this was a close friend, her grandfather still wanted to protect her identity. She watched the hand gestures and also focused on their lips. She heard "two" and "biohazardous" and understood exactly what her grandfather was saying. The men shook hands again, and Keith turned and started walking back toward her. She climbed in and he got in the passenger side.

"Shall we?" He smiled.

"Yes."

Jacqui turned the engine over and backed the truck up enough into a wider spot to turn it around. They drove back to the farm in silence, and she smiled when her grandfather reached over and squeezed her right hand.

"Let's go check on your momma."

She nodded silently.

JACQUI AND KEITH ENTERED THE HOUSE AND WERE PLEASED to find Emma and Carol in the living room, sharing a drink and laughing.

"Wow, it's nice to see how well adjusted you both are." Jacqui studied both their faces, relaxing a little more. "I was worried."

"Well, this definitely helps." Emma held up a glass of wine. "So, who were those people?"

Jacqui and Keith shared a look before taking a seat on the sofa.

"Lionel Whitlock knows I'm alive, and apparently he wants to rectify that."

"You're mother's brother?" Emma asked.

"Yes. A few days ago, I had a man come see me. He told me he used to work for Lionel and had been given a project to find me and find out everything about me. Instead, he gave Whitlock an empty file and provided me with all kinds of interesting information about my uncle." She cringed a little at her own reference. "I figured another person would be hired for the project after the first guy quit, but I had no idea things would unfold this quickly. I definitely never thought he would come after all of you. I am so sorry."

"Hey, this is not on you." Keith reached over and squeezed her hand. "When Emma showed up here all those years ago, she told us the unfortunate conversations she'd overheard in the DeMott house. We understood the dangers and we didn't care. You and Emma were our priority, and you still are."

Jacqui smiled, suddenly feeling overwhelmed with emotion. She stood up and walked over to the wall of books, reading over the various titles to help her regain control over her emotions. Now more than ever, she knew what she had to do.

"I should get going." Jacqui turned around. "I've got a long drive, and I'm already a little tired."

Emma stood and walked over, putting her arms around her.

"You are still the most important thing that's ever come into my life." She pulled back, looking into her daughter's eyes. "I will always love you and want to protect you."

"Thank you," Jacqui whispered, a small break in her voice.

Keith was suddenly next to them. "You take care of yourself and just do what you need to do to survive. And know we're here for you." He leaned forward and kissed her forehead.

"Thank you." She looked up into his eyes. "You'll be happy to know, I do have someone I can call on if I need help."

"Well, that definitely makes *me* feel better." Carol walked over to join them. "Is this that special someone you were referring to earlier?"

Jacqui laughed. "Yes, it is, and I promise to bring him by soon. In the meantime, I've got work to do."

Jacqui stepped away from them and walked toward the door. She turned and looked back to them. "I will call you when it's done. I love you."

She walked out the door, not waiting for a response, knowing it would be overwhelming for her—in a good way.

Jacqui smiled when she saw Chu Long standing next to her truck, looking like a proud teacher.

"You did very well today, *tre em*." He bowed his head.

"Thank you, Chu Long. I appreciated your assistance." She started to get in her truck and stopped. "Hey, I just remembered the three bodies in the barn."

He chuckled. "Consider the matter wrapped." He winked.

"Well, okay then." She opened the driver's-side door.

"You've made me very proud." He smiled at her.

"Thank you."

Jacqui got in her truck and drove slowly out of the driveway. When she pulled out on the main road, she could no longer hold her tears back. She turned up some metal music and let the tears flow, washing away years of pain and frustration. She had been so concerned the Danielses would never accept her if they knew who she really was, and now that they had, she knew she needed to keep them safe. As the last of her pain dried, her thoughts went to how to put an end to Whitlock. *He is done.*

CHAPTER 26

J ACQUI HAD JUST FINISHED BRUSHING HER TEETH AND turned the light off in the bathroom when the alarm for her security cameras chirped at her. Someone was on her property. Probably the team Lionel had sent to take care of her. *This should be fun.*

She checked the cameras, clocking one man on the back side of the property and two more standing in the front, trying to figure out where the door was. She glanced down at her black undies, chuckling to herself when she noticed she was wearing her purple Joker T-shirt. *How poetic.*

Jacqui pulled on her black combat boots and grabbed her belly holster with Bianca, adding a suppressor. She quickly climbed up the ladder mounted on the wall near the bathroom door. She pushed the window all the way open, snagging her spare pair night optical/observation device on the way to the roof. She slipped the goggles on, staying low to scan the grassy area behind her house. She located him about thirty yards out and put one in his chest and one in his throat. He dropped to the ground and she climbed back down the ladder, leaving the NODs in their special hiding place.

She walked back over to her desk and saw the other two men still trying to figure out how to open a door on the front of the building. Jacqui rolled her eyes and chuckled, removing her holster. She set Bianca down and grabbed Rosie, hitting a button to unlock the door in the front of the building. She watched in disbelief when they heard a mechanism behind the wall. They opened the door and slowly stepped inside, chatting among themselves. *Is this the team he sent to kill me? Seriously?*

She shook her head, walking over to the double barn doors in her bedroom. She slowly opened them up, standing there for a moment so they could take her in.

"Hi, can I help you?" Her voice was soft and sweet as she stood there with her right hand on her hip, her weapon pointed down behind her.

Both men allowed their guns to fall to their sides as they stood still, staring up at the half-naked woman wearing a T-shirt and underwear.

"*Damn.* Is that the target?" the taller of the two men asked his partner, his mouth falling open and his eyes widening when he noticed the bottom of her bare breasts peeking out from under the shirt.

"I hope not." The shorter man reached down and adjusted himself. "If it is, I kinda wanna *hit* that before we hit it. You know?"

"Yeah, I agree." The taller man smirked. "Hey, honey, what's your name?"

"Jacqui, but you can call me Karma."

She smiled, quickly bringing her arm forward and shooting the taller man in the face just below his nose. She shot the other man in the right shoulder, causing him to drop his gun and double over, holding his arm. She squatted down and jumped out of the loft to the floor. The second man looked up just in time to see the butt of her gun before it hit him in the forehead. He hit the ground and was out. She picked up his gun and walked around him to check the pulse of the first guy to make sure he was dead. She grabbed his gun, too, and walked over to a small workbench against the wall. She removed the mags and the rounds in the chamber before tucking the weapons away inside a drawer. She picked up a chair and the duct tape, then walked back over to the man who was still alive. She checked his pulse before unbuttoning his shirt. She pulled his body into an upright position so she could squat down and pick him up, placing him in the chair. She removed his shirt and secured his upper body and arms to the back of the chair with tape. She also secured his legs to the front legs of the chair. *So it begins.*

Jacqui walked over to the wall on the right and punched in a code. The pocket door slid open, and she entered her pantry, grabbing a pair of surgical gloves, a set of medical tongs, and sea salt. She headed into the kitchen and filled a large glass of water. She didn't want to keep her guest waiting, so she carried everything at once back out to the barn area and set her tools on a small stainless steel surgical table near the wall. She walked up to the unconscious man, who was moaning a bit, and tossed water in his face, causing his head and body to jerk back in the chair. He looked up at her standing in front of him.

"Welcome back, sunshine." She stared at him for a moment. "Let's chat."

"You *shot* me." He glanced at his partner on the ground near him. "Oh, *man*, is he *dead*?"

"Yep. Now, tell me about the one who sent you."

The man looked back in her direction, his eyes getting bigger when he noticed his shirt was missing and she still wasn't wearing any pants. In fact, she wore just a T-shirt with a set of eyes and a huge red-painted smile that read *The joke's on you,* a black thong, and black combat boots. Damn, he hated irony.

"Forget it. We were just following orders." His eyes roamed over her body, and despite how much pain he was in, he was still aroused by the sight of her.

"I know." She smirked. "But I need the name of the person who gave you the orders."

He looked away, shaking his head. "You might as well just kill me, because there's no way in *hell* you're gettin' anything out of me."

She grinned. "Let's test that theory, shall we?" She winked and turned, walking over to a small folding table that had the gloves, tongs, and salt. She set the glass down and then picked up the table, walking back over with it. She set it down a couple of feet from where he was sitting, close enough for him to see everything on it.

His eyes roamed over everything on top of the table, and fear appeared behind them when he realized what she was going to do next. "Hey, you don't have to do this."

He started struggling in his chair, wincing from the pain of the bullet in his shoulder.

"Actually, I do." She smiled, pulling the gloves on with a snap before she walked back over to him. "I'm pretty sure I already know who sent you." She walked around him counter-clockwise, stopping directly behind him. She leaned forward and whispered in his right ear, "But I *really* wanna hear you say it." She squeezed his injured shoulder, causing him to wince more.

"*Bitch*. That *fuckin'* hurt." His breathing was rapid, and his eyes were slightly glazed. "I'm not tellin' you *shit*, and you can't make me."

"Oh, I do enjoy a challenge."

She walked past him over to the table to dip her left thumb in the water and then in the salt. His eyes traveled over her body, taking in her strong legs and round ass. Who the hell was this woman?

She noticed him studying her and smiled when his eyes got bigger, seeing the large granules of salt on the thumb of her glove. She moved toward him, hesitating for a moment to add to his anxiety.

"You know . . ." She plopped down in his lap, straddling him. " . . . I thought maybe we should clean that wound of yours and see if we can't get that bullet out. We don't want it to get infected, do we?"

He tried leaning back in his chair when she stuck her thumb into the bullet wound and turned it, pushing the salt farther into the broken flesh.

The man winced, attempting to mask his screams of anguish, but failed.

"You can make the pain stop by simply telling me what I want to know." She pulled her thumb out of the bullet hole and smirked. She leaned in toward his right ear and whispered, "The beauty of living this far out is, no one can hear you."

The man grunted and attempted to move his body to relieve the pain.

"*Fuck*." He looked into her eyes, sweat moving rapidly across his forehead and down his face. "Who the *hell* are you, and why does Whitlock want you dead?"

"*Ah*. There it is, thank you." She moved off his lap and back over to the table. "I do appreciate the confirmation."

"*Damn it,*" he whispered under his rapid breathing.

"Now, how much security does he have around him on a daily basis?"

He shook his head, panting a bit. "Forget it."

She smiled and turned back to the table, picking up the salt and the tongs. She poured some salt on the table and dipped the tongs in the water before coating the silicone tips with large granules.

"Let's see if we can't get that pesky bullet out while we continue our conversation." She walked back over to him and sat down hard on his lap.

"Damn it! *No!*" he grunted, shifting back and forth in the chair.

Jacqui gripped his legs with her own and placed her right forearm against the top of his chest, leaning into him. "Hold still, or I'm not going to be able to pull the bullet out. Hey, do you remember that game Operation? I know it was way ahead of our time—well, *mine* anyway. I used to love playing it." She chuckled, maneuvering the tongs in to position. "Now, I'm not gonna lie. This is gonna hurt."

"You *fuckin' bitch*!" he cried out as the instrument was

pushed through the bullet hole, which was significantly smaller than the tips of the tongs.

"Shh . . . I'm trying to work here, and you still haven't answered my question. Now, let's both try to focus, shall we?"

Jacqui pushed the tips in a little deeper, detecting the bullet. When she knew she could easily grab it, she paused a moment, expanding the tongs more than necessary, which tugged internally on the sides of the wound.

"Grr . . . ah . . . FOUR! Four men!" he panted, dropping his head forward, resting it against her right shoulder. "*Please*, please stop."

She gripped the bullet and pulled it out of his body. "Thank you."

She got off his lap and walked back over to the table, setting the tongs and bloody bullet down, along with her gloves. She looked over her shoulder, studying the man in the chair, knowing he didn't have much left in him. She still needed to confirm Whitlock's location for the next few days. She walked toward him, pausing when she heard him mumbling under his breath. She moved around behind him, leaning over his shoulder.

"I just need one more thing from you and then you can go," she whispered. "Where is Whitlock going to be for the next couple of days?"

She leaned in, cradling his chin in her left hand while gently stroking the right side of his face. She listened carefully as he confirmed the location she already knew, his voice just above a whisper.

"Thank you," she whispered back to him before snapping his neck.

Jacqui glanced at the clock on the wall just above the workstation. It was just coming up on midnight. She went inside and ran upstairs to put some pants on. *It's going to be a long night.*

JACQUI ADJUSTED HER MASK AND GLOVES, WATCHING AS THE blue flames of the burn pile stretched up toward the night sky. She'd checked the direction of the wind before dousing a few old rags with isopropyl alcohol and tossing them on the pile. That, coupled with a few soaked rags tucked strategically around the bodies, helped everything ignite quickly, as the smoke and smell were carried across her property, past her house, and toward the main road. Just another perk of living so far out—nobody around to ask why or what the hell you were burning at two in the morning. She was pleased to detect the smell of rain in the air, knowing it would be helpful with downplaying the smell of burning flesh. Georgia never failed to offer spontaneous showers when least expected.

She turned away from the fire and tossed a few supplies back into the empty wheelbarrow. Casting one last glance at the flames that had already been burning for thirty minutes, she lifted the handles and pushed the wheelbarrow back toward the house, smiling as a few drops began falling from the sky. She removed her supplies from the wheelbarrow, leaving it outside to let the rain wash it clean.

Jacqui stepped back into the barn just before the sky really opened up. Three men in the pile tonight; that was a lot. The pile was not a method she had to employ often, but she had definitely fine-tuned the procedure. She'd removed the bullets and, after soaking them to remove all traces of blood, she set them aside to toss into her discharged rounds downstairs. She sorted through and collected their personal effects, taking everything back into the kitchen, setting them on a towel that was spread out on her countertop. She removed all the IDs, credit cards, and cash from the wallets, making separate piles.

Any jewelry would be taken to a pawn shop, and the money for those items, plus whatever cash was in the wallets, would be donated to those less fortunate. Well, less fortunate than herself but more fortunate than the poor bastards who'd ended up on a burn pile.

She grabbed all the IDs and credit cards and ran upstairs, hitting the button on the shredder and running them through. She'd already washed their clothes—what could be salvaged—and now the clothes were ready for the dryer. When they were dry, she'd bag them up with the empty wallets and drop them off in one of those metal clothing bins seen all over town.

She closed the door on the dryer and opened the shower door, turning the water on. Morning for her would come too quickly, considering it was already coming up on 4:00 a.m. She'd left some cat litter on the floor downstairs to soak up the mess, and she would clean it up and add fresh straw across that section of the floor when she got up. The visqueen as a base under a ton of straw just made sense for easier cleanup. She pulled off her clothing and stepped into the shower, allowing the water to drench her from head to toe. By the time Jacqui's head hit the pillow, she fell into a deep sleep, knowing she needed to move fast and put a plan into action.

CHAPTER 27

J ACQUI WAS IN THE KITCHEN REFILLING HER WATER BOT-
tle when a buzz from the gate drew her attention to the
monitor on the wall. She walked over, smiling when she
saw Denner sitting there on his bike.

"Come on up." She pushed the button to unlock the gate.

She grabbed her bottle and moved through the pantry back
out to the center of the barn. The front doors were open, and
she'd been enjoying the fresh air from the early-morning rain.
She'd just finished scooping all the contaminated cat litter and
straw into the wheelbarrow, which was waiting outside to go
back to the burn pile.

She stepped outside the front doors, soothed by the rum-
bling of the Harley's engine. It made her smile—or maybe it
was the sight of him.

Denner parked the bike and turned the engine off. "Afternoon."

"Good afternoon. What brings you by?"

The reason wasn't really important, just that he was there.
Her eyes followed his muscular body while he dismounted

from the bike, the flutter in her stomach causing her smile to broaden.

"I wanted to see what you were up to today."

"Really?" She was acting coy.

"Actually, I just wanted to see you." He removed his helmet and set it on the front of the bike before sauntering over to her. He leaned down, dropping a kiss on her naturally rose-colored lips. "You look a little tired. Late night?"

"You could say that." She glanced around.

Denner's gaze followed hers, and his brow wrinkled. "That smell in the air. Wait, I know that smell. Burnt human flesh."

"Well, maybe there was a new burial down the road. I tell ya, the right wind and you'll be smelling that for a couple of days." She chuckled nervously, although she wasn't sure why.

Denner looked on the ground directly in front of the barn. He noticed two different types of footprints, larger than hers. They were deep, like they had been standing there awhile. The treads were good work boots, and whoever was wearing them were good sized.

He looked around a little more; then saw she was watching him.

"Something you wanna tell me?"

"I'm not sure. Do I?"

"Jacqui, what's going on?" He looked past her into the barn, noticing the straw missing from the center of the floor, and he saw the visqueen underneath.

"Well, Whitlock sent a team to take me out. Obviously, they failed."

"Okay, and I assume they didn't just burst into flame?"

"No, I have a burn pile out back. Their clothes were washed and will be donated, and their jewelry will be pawned. Any cash will also be donated."

"Wow, efficient." He chuckled. "Why didn't you call me?"

"Because in the time it would have taken you to get here, it was done. Well, actually, the guy I held over for enhanced interrogation might have still been around. He really didn't want to cooperate."

She turned and walked back into the barn with Denner following.

"So, you're just finishing the cleanup part?" He grinned.

"Something like that." She walked past him. "I've gotta take a few more things back to the burn pile. You want to come with me?"

"Definitely." He followed her out the front of the barn and over to the east side.

She picked up the handles of the wheelbarrow, moving swiftly toward a far corner of her property. The closer they got, the stronger the smell.

"Oh, damn." Denner squeezed his nostrils a bit, attempting to block some of the smell, but it was too late. He remembered the distinct odor from his military days—it was one you couldn't forget. "How many were there?"

"Three." She set the wheelbarrow down at the edge. She tipped it sideways and allowed the contents to spill over the edge onto the rest of the ashes.

"You know, you're lucky you're surrounded by farmland and cemeteries." He took a step back, studying the perimeter of sand lining the end of the pile. In his own experience, he'd found it to be one of the best ways to keep a fire contained. "It's always surprising to me how strong that smell is even after it rains."

"I agree with you on all counts. I'm not sure what happened to the men on the farm." She looked at him and then realized she hadn't told him. "On my way home from Tennessee, I decided to stop by and visit my adopted family, and it was good I did. Ali was right. Apparently, Whitlock's new hacker had already provided him with everything about me, including Emma's family and their location."

"Are you telling me he sent people to kill them?"

"Exactly. Had it not been for me and Chu Long, they might have all been murdered."

He stepped closer to her and reached out, pulling her into his body. He smiled when he felt her arms wrap around him.

"What's your next move?" He tipped her face up to look at him.

"Research. Strategize. Finish it."

"Count me in."

He leaned down and kissed her softly on the lips.

"I can go get us some food." He stepped away and picked up the handles of the wheelbarrow.

"Well, fortunately, I did some shopping yesterday, and we have everything we need."

They walked back toward the house and worked together, adding more straw to the floor of the barn.

When she was satisfied with the coverage, they went inside and made dinner together.

ENNER CAME BACK UPSTAIRS WITH A COUPLE MORE BEERS. They had been going back over all the information they had on Whitlock from online as well as the file Ali had provided them. She didn't want any more surprises. Jacqui had also taken a moment to review what was found on her, including DMV photos of her and her parents, the name of the company she'd purchased, and her aliases. Guess you can only buy so much anonymity, especially when you have a top-notch hacker involved.

"Find something interesting?" He set a bottle on the desktop near her.

"Thanks." She looked up and smiled. "As a matter of fact, I did. Ali was incredibly thorough in his report. He gave me all of Whitlock's appointments, although the names were coded so I don't really know who Whitlock was meeting on those days. I haven't gotten to the emails Ali included."

Denner pulled up his chair. "That's great. Now you can really see what he's been up to." He glanced over at her, pausing when he saw the look on her face. "Jacqui, what did you find?"

She looked at him, still holding a piece of paper in her hand. "The last job I had in Tennessee was for a Malcolm Bennett. He and Whitlock had attended the same college at the same time. There were months of communication between the two of them and a proposal Whitlock made Bennett to buy his company, which looked to be in financial trouble. According to the emails, Bennett finally agreed to take a meeting with Whitlock and discuss the terms of a sale for the company. Their meeting was last Wednesday afternoon. I got the contract for Bennett Wednesday night, specifically asking for BJ Lock." She looked over at him, a stunned look on her face. "What if Bennett decided at the last minute he didn't want to sell and that pissed Whitlock off?"

"Well, from what you've told me, we know what Whitlock will do if he doesn't get his way." Denner paused, staring down at a piece of paper. "Hey, there's an email here between them with Whitlock talking about how he knew they didn't get along well in college but that he really wanted to help Bennett out." He handed the printed email over to her.

She read through it and shook her head. "What if Bennett had no intention of ever selling to Whitlock? What if Bennett was just wasting his time?" She looked at Denner. "That son of a bitch knowingly hired me to take out Malcolm Bennett, who from what I can tell was not a bad guy, all in the name of getting what he wanted."

"I could see him putting a hit out on someone just out of spite." Denner took a sip of beer.

"*Shit.*"

Jacqui tossed the file down on her desk and stood, walking across the room.

Denner watched in silence, giving her a moment.

"He's still doing it." She turned and faced him. "He's still killing people who get in his way for business."

"We're going to get him."

"'We'?"

"Yeah, we." He stared at her, confused by her response.

"You know, this isn't your problem. You shouldn't feel obligated or anything just because we've been hangin' out."

Right before his eyes, Denner saw Jacqui's walls go up, walls he had managed to get through in the past week. The last thing he wanted was to lose her now.

"Wait, *what*?" He stood and walked over to her. "I'm here for you, to help you do whatever is needed to take this bastard down."

"I'm just saying, if you don't really want to get involved, I would understand." She moved around him, walking over to her dresser and shifting items around without a real purpose.

He walked over and placed his hands on her shoulder, squeezing them gently. He dropped a soft kiss just behind her left ear and whispered, "I'm already involved. I'm here with you researching, trying to help you find anything that will make taking him down easier, because I care about you." He turned her around, lifting her chin with his finger. "I don't want him to hurt you or anyone else you care about. I love you."

Overwhelmed with emotions, she pulled away and walked across the room, looking down at the new straw on the barn floor. She closed her eyes and let its aroma overload her senses as she struggled to breathe. She needed to calm her emotions, which were getting the better of her. She wiped her eyes quickly when she heard him approaching.

"Are you okay?" His voice was soothing and calm.

"The last man who told me he loved me betrayed me

right after I said it back to him. I was devastated. He'd also promised to help me with a mission, and suddenly that also fell through."

"Jacqui, I know you've had a difficult life and you don't trust easily." He paused when she turned to look at him. "But I'm here for you, for whatever you need."

She nodded but her eyes looked stormy and troubled. He reached up and stroked her right cheek. She took a step back from him, and he suddenly saw something behind her eyes he'd never seen before: fear. He waited in silence, knowing she was trying to decide what she should share with him.

"There have been a few times in my life when everything just became too much and I needed a break, when going to the range or sparring with someone just didn't make me feel better. Whenever that would happen, all I wanted was a place to feel safe, where I didn't have to be strong." She looked down into the barn again. "I wanted a man I knew I could trust, who made me feel protected. When it all got to be too much, he would let me climb into his lap and wrap his strong arms around me, shielding me from harm. I'd feel safe enough to shed my armor and lay my weapons down so I could have the purest of moments to heal. So I waited."

"Jacqui . . ." He stepped forward, and she took another step back.

"I thought I'd found that man at one time. I felt protected and safe for the first time in my life." She looked up, and there was anger in her eyes. "Then we had a disagreement, and he used my moment of vulnerability against me, throwing it back at me like a specially forged weapon designed to tear away at my heart and soul."

"So what happened?"

"I shot both of his kneecaps out," she said dryly, wiping her tears away. "We sorta broke up after that."

"Well, sure." He rubbed the side of his head.

She looked up into his eyes. "Look, it's just been a long time since I let someone in after that. I'm scared."

"I understand." He took a step closer, happy when she held her ground. "I am the man who will stand beside you, and will shield and protect you whenever you need."

"I know and I am grateful for that." She smiled.

"Besides, you are the last person I want coming after me if I screw up."

She laughed with her hands on her hips. "Damn straight, mister."

"And, hey . . ." He stepped closer, cupping her face gently in his hands and then kissing her softly. He looked into her eyes. "You don't have to tell me you love me right now."

"Okay."

"We should get some sleep—but first I want to give you something."

"What?" she asked.

Denner took her hand and walked over to the bed. He sat and leaned back against the pillows. He stared into Jacqui's eyes for a moment and then pulled her onto his lap. She slowly leaned forward, melting into his body. He wrapped his strong arms around her, gently rocking as she released years of pain and frustration. After some time, she was quiet, and he realized she was asleep. He gently rolled her over on her side. He studied the face of this woman, now having an understanding of why she didn't let many people in. He brushed a stray hair off her tearstained face, amazed at the vulnerability he'd been privileged to witness. He would do everything in his power to always be there for her and never let her down so she wouldn't have to feel that pain again.

CHAPTER 28

ENNER ROLLED OVER TO FIND HIMSELF ALONE IN BED, then heard the shower. He glanced at the clock, discovering it was coming up on 6:00 a.m. He pulled out his phone and sent a text to George, asking him to open the shop and telling him he was taking the day off. His phone buzzed, and he shook his head at the emoji response George sent over.

He rolled out of bed and walked into the bathroom, not at all surprised when Jacqui popped the shower door open.

"Morning." She smiled, dripping wet.

"Morning, yourself. Mind if I join you?" He started walking forward.

"Not like that." She chuckled at his disappointment. "You need to take off your clothes first." She winked and closed the door.

Denner stripped down and opened the door, stepping into the warm water.

"Soap?" She started reaching for the bodywash.

"Or you could just rub up against me."

He grinned and she cupped her hands together, throwing water at him. He grabbed her and kissed her passionately, lathering her body up with additional soap.

"I've never seen you with your hair down." He winked. "I like it."

"I usually keep it braided because it's easier to manage. But if you play your cards right, mister, I'll start wearing it down more often."

He grinned, pulling her in for a kiss. "Whatever makes you happy."

Denner and Jacqui spent the day together going over the intel for Whitlock and the best way to take him out.

"From what I was told, Whitlock usually has four men around him for protection."

"And you got this from a reliable source?" he asked skeptically.

"Well, the guy was screaming a lot, but yes, I would have to say, in the end, he was definitely telling the truth." She couldn't help but laugh from the look on his face.

"Enhanced interrogation?"

"Yes."

"Well, okay. Knowing what I know about you now, I know you were thorough." He chuckled.

"Indeed, I was."

"Well, I can assure you Whitlock has at least one guy we don't know about." He looked at her.

"'Cause that's how *you'd* do it." She smirked.

"Exactly."

"Okay, well I'm sure since none of the men from the two previous hits ever reported in, he'll be taking extra steps to cover his ass."

"So what are you thinking?" Denner sat back in his chair. He could practically see the wheels turning behind her eyes.

"I say we go now." She stood up and walked over to her dresser. She opened a drawer and removed a few articles of clothing.

"Right now?" Denner glanced at the clock on the nightstand. "It's three thirty in the afternoon."

"Exactly. According to his schedule, he will be in meetings until five thirty. I want this finished by six p.m."

He nodded. "Okay."

"I've gotta change. I'll meet you downstairs in ten minutes."

"You got it."

Denner headed downstairs and stepped outside to grab a few items from his saddlebags.

Jacqui changed into the leggings and long-sleeved undershirt she wore under her racing suit. She stepped into the bathroom and wound her braid into a tight bun at the base of her neck, clipping it into place. She slipped her racing boots on and grabbed her tact vest, making sure it was loaded up with all the necessary items for contract jobs. She walked back over to her workstation, pulling the pictures of her parents out from under the pile of papers. She studied their faces for a moment, tracing the images with her fingertips, feeling her resolve building inside her. She set the photos back down on the table and grabbed a copy of the blueprints that were in the file. Then she saw the note with the phone number on it. Well, he did say call if she needed any help.

She dialed the number and waited.

"Hello?"

"Ali, it's Jacqui Bleu."

"Hey, what's up?"

"I was just wondering if you still had access to the DeWhit Holdings security feed."

"As a matter of fact, I do. What do you need?" His glee came through the phone.

"I need you to disrupt the security feed for the rest of the evening. Can you do that?"

"As long as this means you're finally putting that bastard in the ground."

"That I am. Can you do it?"

"Anything for you." He chuckled. "What kind of window are we looking at?"

"Can you pull it down at five thirty-eight and create a false loop?"

"I can. In fact, let's make this look like a systems failure. I'll loop the camera until midnight and also deactivate all the alarm systems, including the silent alarm."

"Thank you."

"Oh, one last thing. Margie, Whitlock's assistant, should be gone for the day by four thirty. She goes to a senior swim every Monday, although that's not your biggest issue."

"And what might that be?"

"The two security guards down in the lobby, and recently

Whitlock added an armed guard just outside the elevator upstairs around the corner from his office."

"Good to know, thanks."

"I'll call you when it's done."

"Ali, thank you."

"Hey, I'm just happy to help. Later."

The call ended.

Jacqui grabbed her racing jacket and balaclava and headed downstairs with the layout of the building. She found Denner in the kitchen, checking his weapons. He smiled when he noticed her tact vest and all the gear, and then he saw her racing pants.

"You're a little dressed up for your Harley, aren't ya?" He tucked his M17 back into his chest rig, winking at her.

"I'm not taking the Harley." She laid her jacket on the island and her balaclava on top. "I'm taking Della. Oh, I need your phone."

He pulled his phone and handed it to her. She typed in the address to DeWhit Holdings, then handed it back to him.

"Thanks."

"I just spoke with Ali, and he is pulling the security feed down for the rest of the night, plus killing the alarm system." She laid the blueprints for the building down on the countertop. "I'm looking to breach around five forty p.m. I'll go in here on the south side, through the service and maintenance entrance. I'll take the service elevator up and go through the air duct, dropping into this storage closet near the stairs and the main elevator."

"Good." He looked at the floorplan.

"He also confirmed two security guards down in the lobby and one armed guard just outside the elevator upstairs around the corner from Whitlock's office." Jacqui picked up her balaclava, slipped it over her head, and pulled on her racing jacket.

"Sounds good. Hey, who's Della?"

She grinned, adjusting her jacket and moving down the hall to the closet under the stairs with Denner following her. She opened the door and flipped on the light.

His mouth dropped open and he stared, watching her wheel a bike out from the closet.

"That's a Ducati Panigale V4."

"Yes it is, which means you're gonna need at least a thirty-minute head start." She dropped the stand and grabbed the helmet from inside the closet, flipping the light off and closing the door.

He pulled his leather jacket on, unable to take his eyes off the bike.

"Seriously. You've got thirty minutes to get a good lead on me, and then I start without you." She zipped her jacket halfway up, adjusting the collar and her vest underneath.

He took a few steps toward her. "Okay, that seems fair. I see you ordered a comfort fit on your jacket for all your accessories," he teased.

"Gotta have my weapons and armor." She winked. "Hey, are you . . ."

He smiled, pulling up the tail of his button up shirt to show he was also wearing a vest. "You know that suit doesn't buy you much in the way of camouflage."

"Then I'll have to be fast." She smirked.

"See you there." He leaned over and kissed her.

Denner walked out the door and headed for their destination.

Jacqui pulled Rickie off the Ducati, reloading the shotgun and then reattaching it under the seat. She sat down at the island for a moment and stared across the room at the empty tank, reflecting on everything she'd lost in her lifetime because of Whitlock. *It ends tonight.*

She stood and walked down the hall, past her bike, and opened the door. She wheeled it out and locked everything up. She started the bike and headed down the driveway.

Jacqui drove the Ducati down a side road, pulling it over into an area with heavy foliage. She cut the engine and pulled her helmet off, setting it on the front of the bike. She tapped the call button on her watch, pulling her monocular from her vest.

"Go for Denner." He pulled his compact binoculars and looked toward the front doors.

"What's your twenty?" She moved off the bike and crouched down in the brush, looking up at Whitlock's floor.

"I'm about fifty yards from the beautiful glass doors on the front of the building."

"What do you see?"

"I see the two guards on the desk, both with sidearms and Tasers, and with keys for locking and unlocking the doors."

"Okay, and we know of the one outside the elevator upstairs, if Ali's intel is correct. I figure if there is an extra, he'll be close to Whitlock."

"Yep, the extra security we figured he might have." Denner exhaled.

She glanced at the time. 5:38 on the nose. "Oh, call you right back." She ended the call right as Ali's call came in. "Hello?"

"All systems down."

"Thanks."

She called Denner back. "All systems are down."

"Got it. I'll go in through the front doors and take those guards out. Then I'll take the elevator up and take out the other one, which should hopefully clear a path for you. Listen for a double knock on the storage door as I move past it heading down the hall," he explained.

"Then I'll slip out and into the stairwell."

"If there is personal security with Whitlock, I'll create a distraction down the hall, draw him out. Then you slip in."

"Copy that," Jacqui replied.

"Hey, maybe when this is done, you'll finally let me take you to dinner."

"Seriously? We're having this conversation now?"

He chuckled into the phone. "Just calming your nerves."

Damn, he was right. "Nicely done." She glanced at her watch. "T-minus ninety seconds."

"Copy that. I'm going in."

Jacqui slipped out of the bushes and raced over to the service entrance. She pulled her cylinder drill and opened the lock door, moving quickly down the hallway to the service elevator. She rode it up to the top floor, then climbed up through the ceiling. She crawled through the air duct and dropped into the storage closet. Then she waited.

DENNER WALKED ACROSS THE PARKING LOT AND ENTERED the building.

"Can I help you?" One of the guards walked toward him.

Denner smiled. "Wow, this is a beautiful building. Do you happen to know who the architect was?" He looked up, pointing at the beautiful etching in the panes of the higher windows, slowly turning his back to the guards and pulling the suppressor from his left pocket. "I mean, this is simply incredible. You just don't see this much pride and craftsman-ship anymore." He unzipped his jacket and pulled his M17, adding the suppressor while still admiring the lobby with his back to the guards.

"I'm sorry, sir, but we are closing for the evening. If you could maybe come back tomorrow . . ."

"Sorry." Denner turned, shooting the guard in front of him twice in the head and then shot the one who stood up behind the desk twice. He checked for a pulse, grabbed the keys, and moved back over to the doors, locking them. He turned, moving through the lobby, grabbing the guard's arm and pulling him out of sight before hitting the button for the elevator. He stepped on and hit the button for the top floor. He pressed his body into the corner, and when the doors opened, he held the button to keep the doors from closing. He waited for the guard to poke his head in and then he shot him, catching the body before it dropped. He laid the body down inside the car and stepped out, moving quickly toward the storage closet. He gave the door a double knock and kept moving down the hall.

He glanced over his shoulder and saw Jacqui slipping through the door to the stairs.

Denner ducked into a conference room halfway down the hall, rolling under a table. Now he just needed to wait, knowing security would check the floor after the elevator chimed and no one appeared.

PHILLIPS, YOU ARE HERE BECAUSE I'M NOT SURE WHEN SHE will show up; I just feel like it will be soon." Whitlock took a long sip from his almost-empty glass. "Neither of the teams I sent to take her family and her out ever reported back, which means she was able to take them all out. Damn, that little bitch is good."

"Sir, I believe she might already be here." Phillips pulled his weapon.

"What makes you say that?" Whitlock sat forward in his chair.

"I heard the bell for the elevator, but no one is here." He stared at his boss for a moment. "I'm going to check it out."

"Good, yes—go, please."

Whitlock watched Phillips leave his office before walking back over to his bar to pour himself another drink. He couldn't believe for the first time in his life he was actually scared, and of all things, his niece.

Phillips walked out of the office and around the corner to the elevator. He hit the button and when the doors opened, he saw the guard inside on the floor. He checked the man's pulse to confirm he was dead. He stepped back out and walked back into Whitlock's office.

"The guard out here is down. I'm going to sweep the rest of the floor."

He didn't wait for his boss to acknowledge; he just moved quickly down the hall, checking every room.

JACQUI WATCHED FROM THE SMALL WINDOW IN THE DOOR TO the stairs. She pulled her weapon, ready if the man decided to come through the door. Instead, she watched as he moved down the long hall. She cracked the door and heard as he opened every conference room door as he went. She wasn't sure where Denner was, but she figured this was her chance.

She stepped into the hallway and moved quickly across the floor, stepping into Whitlock's office just as he was finishing his drink. He looked up and actually smiled. *Must be the liquor.*

"My God, look at you. You are a perfect blend of your mother and father." He paused. "Hello, Jacqueline."

"Whitlock." She held her weapon down by her right leg, staring at him.

Denner heard the door to the conference room open and saw as a man peered around the room, a man he recognized. *Damn it!* Jon Phillips. The man was a psychopath, and not just because Denner thought so. He was booted after he'd failed his last psych eval. Not that the answers he gave couldn't get him a job in another department. It was his reaction to no longer being allowed to do what he loved that set him off. Phillips had disappeared overnight after being asked to take some time off and think about his options. Guess he'd decided to give it a go in the private sector. Denner definitely needed to get him before he got Jacqui.

Phillips heard the voices down the hall and moved quickly toward Whitlock's office.

"You've been rather industrious—and at such a young age. Business owner, bounty hunter, and a contract killer." He smirked. "Do you think your parents would be proud of what you've become?"

"Don't talk about my parents." She could feel her anger rising to the surface.

He chuckled, fueling her anger. "Only twenty-three years old. It's a shame you will never make it to twenty-four."

Jacqui heard the hammer click on a gun behind her. She glanced over her shoulder to see a man standing there, his gun held tightly to his chest but ready to point it directly at her head.

"Aw, thank you, Phillips. As always, your timing is perfect." Whitlock's smug look made her ill.

"Killing me is not the right answer here." She smiled. "I have already sent a file to someone I trust. If I don't call him by tomorrow morning, he will release everything to the press, and although I might not be around to enjoy the show, you'll still be done. And then all this bullshit won't matter."

"Well, that sounds impetuous; of course, you are young so I don't think you really know what it takes to make it long term in the business world. It takes sacrifice and determination."

"That doesn't mean killing off your family members who don't agree with you." She took a step forward.

"Okay, well, clearly you're not going to listen, so, Phillips, if you would . . ."

Jacqui jumped when she heard a zip through the air, then realized she hadn't been shot. Phillips was on the floor, the contents of his head showing. She turned to see Denner standing in the doorway.

"Man, that guy was always an asshole." He winked, and she turned back to face her uncle.

Fear washed over Whitlock's face when he realized he was all alone now.

"Look, your father was being completely unreasonable. I was a visionary, knowing what the merger could do for us, for our company. We were all going to be richer than we were. It was a winning situation."

Jacqui shook her head in disgust. "All this over money?"

"No, not just money. It was a higher status in the business community, something anyone in our position would aspire to—or at *least* they should." He sighed, realizing his passion was getting the better of him. "Look, you're just a small business owner, maybe you just don't understand the business side of things on a larger scale and the sacrifices that need to be made. Perhaps I could explain—"

Jacqui fired a single shot, hitting him squarely between the eyes. She watched his body crumple to the floor, making a loud thud behind his desk. She walked toward the desk and put two more in the man's chest before lowering her gun and looking at Denner.

"There wasn't anything he could've said to save his ass." Jacqui put her weapon away.

"I understand." He studied her for a moment. "How do you feel?"

"Hungry." She shrugged, moving toward the door.

Denner chuckled. "How about takeout and a long shower?"

"Okay."

He followed her out of the office, pushing the button for the elevator. They waited in silence, stepping over the body inside when the doors opened.

"So, what are you going to do with your shares in the company?" he asked.

"Well, according to what I read online, the last company they merged with would like to buy the rest of the shares, so I'm thinking about selling. Guess I do need to call Steele after all."

"You mean, you were bluffing in there?"

"Yep." She looked up, watching the buttons light up as they counted down.

"Nice. You know, you could hold on to the shares for supplemental income," he suggested.

"Hmm. It's a thought."

"So, *now* what?"

"No idea. Maybe buy some more fish."

"You sure that's such a good idea?" Denner teased.

"Not really." Jacqui sighed and smiled. "But it's a place to start."

WEAPONS AND RIDES KEY

JACQUI'S WEAPONS

"Bianca" - Beretta 96A1 12 round/.40 FMJ

"Black Betty" - Walther PPK .380 - Primary Weapon for contract jobs

"Black Dahlia" - SOG Kukri Machete

"Brandi" - SOG Pillar Blackout knife

"Ed" - 16" auto retractable striking stick

"Freddie" - SOG Field knife

"Ivy" - Hand Whip chain bracelet

"Kiki" - SOG Kiku folding knife

"Papi" - Switchblade

"Rickie" - Maverick 88 Cruiser - strapped under the seat on Ducati

"Rosie" - Sig Sauer P365/.380-Rose - Daily Weapon

"Sparky" - Vipertek Flashlight/Taser

JACQUI'S RIDES

First Truck - '63 Chevy K10

Second Truck - '78 Chevy K10

Ducati Pangali V4 with blue fairing

Harley "Fat Boy"

DENNER'S WEAPONS

M17 9mm

Desert Eagle .50 cal

DENNER'S RIDES

Harley Heritage Classic

ACKNOWLEDGMENTS

Thank you to everyone who follows and supports me.

Cocoa Bean, thank you for sharing your
expertise and experience with me.

Stephanie, thank you for being such a fan and
for the idea of the weapons page.

Andrew, thank you for the fish.

ELIZABETH ANNE GREY

 was born in Dallas, Texas, and grew up in Snohomish, Washington, a small town north of Seattle. She has enjoyed writing throughout her life, whether it be poetry, short stories, or full novels. One of her favorite hobbies is research, which is surprising because as a child, getting her to read a book was almost impossible.

She enjoys telling stories that capture the heart, as well as the imagination, while drawing the reader in with real-life experiences to develop a bond with them. Armed with a sharp wit and dark sense of humor, she loves taking her readers on a ride, with murder/mystery as a common thread through different genres.

When she's not writing, Elizabeth enjoys action movies, comedies, and procedural dramas.

You can visit her site www.darkcitrine.net, where you can also find her social media pages.

www.ingramcontent.com/pod-product-compliance
Lightning Source LLC
Chambersburg PA
CBHW020733020826

48980CB00016B/164